Christmas With The Millers

A Bridgeport Holiday

A Novella by Quasia

Copyright © 2020 Quasia Little
Published by Major Key Publishing
www.majorkeypublishing.com

ALL RIGHTS RESERVED.

Any unauthorized reprint or use of the material is prohibited. No part of this book may be reproduced or transmitted in any form or by any means, electronic, or mechanical, including photocopying, recording, or by any information storage without express permission by the publisher.

This is an original work of fiction. Names, characters, places and incidents are either products of the author's imagination or are used fictitiously and any resemblance to actual persons, living or dead is entirely coincidental.

Contains explicit language & adult themes suitable for ages 16+

To submit a manuscript for our review, email us at submissions@majorkeypublishing.com

Synopsis

In the finale, Jade and Nasir finally agree on a wedding date. But some things may cause them to cancel it. Nasir is hiding a secret that can ruin his life and the family he built with Jade. His mother Miranda isn't too fond of his fiancée and does everything she can to plant seeds of doubt in his mind. Will he listen to the woman who was never there for him or stick by the love of his life?

Jade is feeling insecure about herself after having two kids, and her soon to be mother-in-law only makes matters worse. Nasir ignores her complaints about his mother to keep peace in the house. When she runs into Dior at the mall, her whole world stops. She knows Nasir is hiding something but has no idea what it is. Will Jade and Nasir finally get their happy ending?

Chapter One

Jade

I hated the way my body looked in clothes. I was dressed for the gym; stretch marks covered my waist and butt. When I gave birth to Cameron last year, I snapped back. It wasn't until I got pregnant with Callie that I noticed the weight gain. My second pregnancy was different than the first. All of my time went to my son and preparing to have my daughter, so I didn't have time to work out, and I ate like shit. Nasir tried his best, but he wasn't a good cook, so I was the one who did everything. He's been on me about finding a nanny, cook, and housekeeper. Growing up, my mother handled everything and still had a successful career. I would feel like a failure if I had to get help.

Nasir wasn't taking no for an answer and had his mother coming to help. They worked on their relationship once Cam was born. Honestly, it was a good idea at first, but I couldn't stand her ass. It was wonderful they were working on their relationship. In the beginning, she was cool, but she tried to tell me how to raise my children. I didn't need any help from someone who wasn't always a great mother. Nasir practically raised himself and now she was trying to tell me what to do. All I needed was her help watching them while I ran to the store or when I took a shower. I did everything else myself. Miranda had one more time to say or do something slick before I cursed her ass out. She's been staying with us for a few months and it was time for her to take her ass home.

My daughter turned two-months last week, and I needed to get my ass in the gym. Our wedding was set for Christmas 2020. In my mind, I always wanted a spring wedding decorated with hues of light pink, cream, and rose gold. Since I got pregnant, we had to change the date. I refused to be a pregnant bride. Christmas was my favorite time of the year, so it made sense to do it that day. No one I knew ever had a wedding on Christmas.

Walking downstairs I grabbed a protein shake since I skipped breakfast. Nasir had something to do, so Miranda agreed to keep the children until he made it home. If it was up to me, I would wait for him to come home. She liked to act like a super grandma in Nasir's presence, but when he left, she would do a complete 360.

"I don't understand you new mothers. Instead of worrying about how you look, you need to sit in the house and be a mother," Miranda said to me.

Turning around, I looked at her. I was about to say something, but Nasir walked in. She was saved by the bell. This is the shit I hated about her. I wanted to tell my mother about everything she's been doing so she could put her in her place. As much as I wanted to, I just couldn't. I wanted us to all get along, but if my mother were to say something to her, I know for a fact it would end with Miranda getting dragged around the house. My mother was a businesswoman, but she still had a little hood in her. You know that saying, *You can take the girl out the hood, but not the hood out of the girl.* That applied to my mother.

"I came back just in time. Let me walk you to the car," Nasir said, grabbing my hand.

"You see your mother standing here right?"

"Hey, ma. I'll be right back, and we can talk."

Grabbing my hand again, we walked outside. I was quiet. Miranda and her comments always got under my skin. We walked over to my 2020 Mercedes G-Wagon and he opened the door for me. Pulling me close to him, he planted a kiss on my lips.

"Try not to be in the gym all day either. You don't even need to lose weight; you're perfect the way you are. Plus, it's going to be a waste since we're having another baby after the wedding."

Looking at him like he was crazy, I pulled away from him. "Another baby? You got me messed up if you think we're having another one so soon. Callie wasn't even planned, but you can't keep your hands to yourself," I huffed.

"I told you I wanted a house full of kids and you agreed."

"We can but let me give my body a break. In a few more years, we can try again. Let me get out of here, so I can get back home and cook dinner," I told him. "Oh and tell your mother to watch her comments too before I pop her in the mouth."

"What did she say now?" he sighed.

"Never mind, I can already tell you're going to get an attitude. I'll be back later."

I put on my Nicki Minaj playlist and pulled away from the house. Not wanting to think about Nasir wanting to keep me barefoot and pregnant and his bitch ass mother anymore, I rapped along to "Move Ya Hips" and danced in my seat. Pulling up to the gym, I got out of the car and walked towards the entrance. Before I walked in, I remembered something.

"Oh, shit, my mask," I sighed.

This COVID shit was killing me. I couldn't wait for it to be over. I jogged back to my car to grab my face mask and shield just in case I needed to pull my mask down. The gym I went to was very small and clean. It was privately owned by my trainer Jill and her boyfriend. I'd never met him but all she did was talk about him. All I knew was is his name started with a D.

"Welcome. Would you like to purchase something to drink before you start your workout?" the receptionist said.

"No thank you." I smiled.

Walking over to the elliptical machine, I got on to start my thirty minutes of cardio before it was time for my session with Jill. On the days I didn't come to the gym, I liked to jog around the neighborhood with Kiya. She stopped about a month ago since they were trying for a baby. The doctor suggested she stop working out to prevent any miscarriages. I was excited for her and anything she needed, I would gladly help her.

Thirty minutes later, I wiped the machine down. Walking over to the private room, I stopped and stood back when I noticed Jill sitting on her boyfriend's lap, kissing him. To give them their privacy, I went to get a drink of water. When I got back, she stood up and I couldn't believe who her boyfriend was. I tried walking away to avoid an awkward moment.

"Jade, give me a few, and I'll be back," Jill said.

"I knew that name was familiar. How have you been?" Donovan asked me.

"Great! I have two kids now. A boy and a girl. I'm also getting married this Christmas," I replied.

"Wow! Two kids. Congratulations." He smiled. "Who's the lucky guy?" he asked.

"Nasir. Remember the one who came to prom with me?" I reminded him.

"Oh yeah. He was cool. It was nice running into you. See you at home, babe." He kissed Jill on the cheek.

We walked into the private area and started setting up. Jill seemed preoccupied, not her usual, talkative self. She was one of the black girls who acted like a dumb blonde and talked all the damn time, but she was very sweet. I even invited her to my wedding which was probably a mistake since she's Donovan's girlfriend, and he more than likely will be her plus one.

"I don't mean to be unprofessional, but can I ask you a question?" she asked.

As a female, I know how our minds work. She was probably coming up with all different types of scenarios in her head. What I had with Donovan was over with and has been for years. I never even thought about him anymore.

"Sure. Go ahead." I looked at her.

"How do you know my Donovan?"

"We used to date in high school." I kept it real with her.

"Was it serious?"

"Look, Jill, I dated him my freshman year and half of sophomore year. We haven't talked since high school. In all honesty, I thought he was dead or something. I don't know, I never think of him."

"Dead? Don't y'all have the same friends?" she laughed.

"I hated him for a long time and absolutely not. We never hung out with the same people."

"One more question. Why did you break up?"

"He cheated on me and got the girl pregnant. Well, the baby turned out not to be his, but you get the point." I shrugged.

I was tired of talking about my situation with Donovan. That was old news.

"Wow! I hope he's changed." She had a worried look on her face.

"I'm sure he did. That happened when we were kids. About ten years ago. People change. I think he did that because for the first time, he was getting a lot of attention. During senior year, he calmed down a lot. Don't worry, girl." I pat her on the shoulder.

"Thanks for that. I get a little insecure sometimes, and you're beautiful. If he can cheat on you then I have no hope."

"We all have insecurities. I hate the pudge on my stomach and my stretch marks. I've been having a hard time not having my pre-baby body. Look at how big my thighs and ass got as well. If I wanted to take the easy route, I would be getting surgery." I laughed.

***

We couldn't go out to brunch, so we sat in Kiya's backyard with the kids. August in Connecticut was brutal. I couldn't take the heat, especially dealing with two kids. Cam's always running off somewhere, so I was chasing him with a baby in my arms. For the most part, Callie was a good baby until her chunky self-wanted to eat. It's like she'll see you making her bottle and start screaming louder. I breastfed her at night only; most of the time I pumped it so she would get used to being away from me.

"That lil nigga bad as fuck. Whew, chile," Crystal said, fanning herself.

"Bitch, I know you ain't talking when your son ate the communion juice and crackers at church then threw up. That is baby Satan. Had the priest ready to throw holy water."

"I was waiting for his head to start twisting around," Ava said.

"Y'all gon' leave my baby alone."

"You started it. Crystal, you know your son worse than any of the kids. Grandma won't even keep him, and she loves the kids," Kiya replied.

"My son is not bad. He just misses his father…. Hold on," Crystal said, picking up her phone. "Bye, bitches, I have to go. My man is waiting for me."

"Bye," we said in unison.

"I don't see how y'all can be around her all day," Ava laughed.

"Shit, I don't have a choice, that's my family," Kiya said.

"I'm barely around her crazy ass," I replied.

"Enough about her. Did you pick a place for us to go on our girl's trip?" Kiya asked me.

"It's between Greece or Bali."

"I think we should go to Bali. The Kardashian's went, and I'm trying to take pictures with elephants and shit. That's the last trip I'll be able to take," Kiya said.

"Oh, and we can play with tiger cubs. I'm down with going to Bali."

"Okay, I'll have my assistant plan everything."

"Look at you talking about your *assistant*. You're too funny. But Zeek is waiting for me. I'll talk to you later," Ava said.

After she left, I had to tell Kiya about running into Donovan and the problems I'd been having with Nasir's mother. I like to keep things to myself and that's no good. Nasir always seemed to have an attitude and didn't want to talk about anything that came to his mother. Now that Ava went home, I made sure she was gone before telling Kiya about everything.

"Guess who I ran into the other day?"

"Who?"

"Donovan."

"Where the hell did you see him? It's been years since I heard from him and Tommy," she said.

"Remember my trainer Jill? Well, anyways, she was booed up with her man and when they walked out, I talked to him for about a minute. That's her man. They both own the gym where I work out. She was asking me about our relationship."

"Don't nobody want his ass. You're about to be married to a millionaire. That little gym money can't do anything for you." She twisted up her face.

"Period!" I laughed.

"What he look like now?" she asked.

"Honestly, he's still fine as hell with his smooth chocolate skin. I still can't stand his ass though." I rolled my eyes.

"We should have jumped his ass."

"And don't get me started on Nasir's bitch of a mother."

"I thought you liked her. What happened?" she asked me.

"She's always saying slick shit to me and complaining about me not taking care of my children when Nasir isn't around. But let him come back, and it's Super Granny time. I should slap that bitch."

"Let's jump her ass then. What is she saying?"

I explained everything to her. From the time she told me Nasir should have found a woman who put her children first to her telling him I always leave them with her.

"I know that lying ass bitch didn't say that? The mother who let her underage son fend for himself by selling drugs at a young age. The mother who just started coming around. I just know you're lying, Jade," Kiya fumed.

"On my kids that lady on some bullshit."

"And what did Nasir say about his lying ass mama?" she asked.

"Every time I bring it up, he gets an attitude and does not want to talk about it. I stopped telling him. There is no reason to," I sighed.

"Jade, you need to sit him down and have a serious conversation. Don't just tell him about it whenever you see him and don't get an attitude. Just have a nice, civilized conversation."

"What? You didn't tell me to run away and stay at a hotel for a month?" I joked.

"You got too many damn kids to be trying to pack up and run away with. If it was just you then I would say pull a runaway bride on his ass."

"This is not a movie, and I'm not Julia Roberts." I laughed. "I get what you're saying though."

"That's your house to kick her ass out. Nasir has enough money to get her a little condo or something. Heem's mother is cool as hell, so I wouldn't mind, but she needs to go."

Later that day, I was home preparing dinner. I was on a keto diet so I couldn't have carbs and sugar. Tonight's dinner was creamy garlic Tuscan chicken over a sauteed spinach, and I made mashed potatoes for Nasir and Cameron since I couldn't eat it. I also fried a few pieces of chicken on the side for them. Nasir loved this salmon recipe, so I knew he was going to devour it. He's been watching what he eats too since the wedding was coming up, and he already had his tux.

I sat Cam in his highchair so he could eat. His bedtime was in another hour, and I wanted him to eat so he could get his bath. He acted up something terrible today, and I was ready for him to take his behind to sleep. Callie was in her MamaRoo watching me move around the kitchen while listening to Chloe and Halle's new album *Ungodly Hour*. My favorite song so far was "Forgive Me". Once he was finished, I cleaned his high-chair, and we made our way upstairs. I bathed him and got him dressed, so I could read his bedtime story. Every night, he needed a warm cup of milk and a book to put him to sleep. Callie was up next. After her bath, I sat in the rocking chair breastfeeding her. This was our bonding time. Singing her favorite lullaby, she was out like a light. Looking at my phone, I noticed it was going on 7:30 p.m. I couldn't eat after 8, so I decided not to wait for Nasir.

I ate my dinner then went to shower. My nights ended early because I had to get up during the middle of the night to feed Callie. I was thankful Cameron slept through the night and got up almost every day around 9:00 a.m. Nasir still wasn't home, so I decided to call him. His phone went to voicemail. I couldn't wait any longer, so I fell asleep. The next morning, Nasir wasn't in bed. I went to the bathroom to pee and handle my morning hygiene. I wondered where the hell was my man. When I was finished, I went into Callie's room. Nasir was in there changing her diaper. He handed her to me so I could feed her.

"Where were you last night?" I asked him.

"Ummm... I was out with Zeek," he stuttered.

Squinting, I looked at him. Not wanting to start an argument so early in the morning, I let it go. I would ask him about it another time.

Chapter Two

Nasir

I felt Jade's eyes on me as I moved around Callie's nursery. I can admit I was moving suspiciously, but I couldn't look into her face and lie to her. She meant too much to me. When we first met, I had never been in a committed relationship, but it was something about her that made me fall in love with her. We'd been through so much shit over the years, but I was finally getting it right. Well, *we* were because Jade pulled some bullshit as well. We were going to be married in a few months. I spared no expense giving Jade the wedding she wanted and deserved. Our children were happy and healthy. The house we lived in was like something you see in a movie. I had enough money to upgrade Jade's cars every year if she wanted to.

We were extremely blessed, but something was threatening to end our happiness. I struggled with wanting to tell Jade. I had just found out myself. My secret would destroy her and our family. I've been staying out all night and leaving early to avoid her. She was the love of my life. I couldn't live without her. Since we got back together two years ago, we haven't argued or raised our voices. Everything was copacetic. Maybe it was that way because of the storm that was coming.

Jade walked out with Callie in her arms. It was almost time

for Cameron to wake up, so I went into his room. The covers were thrown off of him and his legs hung off the bed. I laughed because his ass slept wild as hell. Somedays I liked to take a nap with him, but I would end up getting up to move into another bed. His feet would be on my head most of the time. He was a wild child. My grandmother said Jade must have acted that way when she was his age because I was always calm as a child. I still was.

"Cam, wake up," I whispered into his ear.

He rubbed his eyes. "Morning, Papa," he smiled.

I picked him up to go sit him on the potty. We were trying to have him potty-trained early. Jade was complaining about having two kids in diapers. Once we were finished, we went downstairs. His food was sitting on his highchair.

"Do you need me to help you out today?" I asked Jade.

"You can do what you always do and leave all day. I can handle my children!" she snapped.

"It's too early in the morning to have an attitude," I told her.

"She always likes this. Try being here all day with her," my mother said.

"You know the fuck what!" Jade yelled, pointing her finger at my mother.

Grabbing her wrist, I pulled her into one of the rooms. Something has been up with her and I couldn't figure out what it was. She's been snappy and lashing out.

"Why are you raising your voice at my mom? She didn't say anything wrong."

"Are you fucking serious? You did not pull me in here to check me about what I said to that witch. I've been telling you for months how she's been saying a bunch of bullshit to me, but you don't ever say shit to her!" she shouted, mushing me.

"Stop calling her out her name. We all need to sit down and talk."

"I'm not talking to her. That is your mother, so that is your job. While you're talking to her, you can keep your children too. I'll be back later." She stormed away.

A few minutes later, she came out in her gym clothes and walked out of the house. Walking over to the window, I looked as she stopped at the truck and slammed the door. Shaking my head, I grabbed both of the kids and headed to their playroom. Callie was in her swing while Cam ran around playing with all of the toys.

"I don't see how you can allow her to just up and leave when the kids need her. She's still breastfeeding. Are you sure she's only going to the gym? That is her excuse for everything. Always leaving out wearing those tight workout clothes," my mother said.

"Yes, she's going to the gym. Our wedding is in a few months."

"I think it's too soon to get married. You're still young. What's the rush?"

"Ma, I've been with Jade since she was seventeen years old, and she's twenty-five now. Trust me, it's time to get married. We're not getting any younger," I told her.

"I don't want you to rush into something. I haven't been the best mother, but I know you were never the type to be in a relationship. Just don't get married to call it quits later," she said before walking out.

My mother was worried about the wrong things. I was getting married if it was the last thing I did. Jade was my everything, and I needed to tell her about the shit I've been going through.

***

I sat talking to Zeek about what I was going through. He was older than us, so I liked to talk to him about certain things.

"I know everything isn't confirmed, but you need to tell her about it. You know how Jade is. She would rather know the truth before it comes out and you didn't tell her. Remember in 2013 when Ronnie told her about the baby, and her ass moved away for five years. Don't lie to her, Nas," Zeek said to me.

"I'm going for the appointment tomorrow. Once I get the results, I tell her," I sighed.

"Good luck with that shit, man. But let's talk about this wedding trip. Where are we going? The women are headed to Bali in a few weeks, and I think we should go at the same time."

"I've been trying to think of where we could go and ride dirt bikes and shit. I want to have fun and shit we don't normally do."

"I want to go scuba diving and shit."

"We did that in the Maldives, and it was fun as hell. I don't mind doing that again. How about Mexico? You can do that there, plus we can rent ATV's and go zip-lining through the jungle."

"See you had me up until the jungle," he laughed.

"Nigga, you scared, and we didn't even get there. It's going to be fun," I told him. "But let me get home to Jade. She's been complaining about me not being home to help her out."

I pulled up to the house and my mother was stomping out. Not wanting to know the reason, I stayed in the car until she pulled off. Jade would be spazzing and I didn't feel like hearing her mouth. I had a headache. After sitting in the car for a few minutes, I got out and dragged my feet. When I walked inside, Jade was nowhere to be found. The house was so quiet, you could hear a pin drop. I checked the kid's rooms, and they weren't in there. *Did she leave the house?* When I got to our room, Cam and Callie were in there watching TV.

"Cam, where is mommy?" I asked him.

He pointed towards the bathroom door. After checking them, I walked in. Jade was sitting on the toilet with her head in her hands, crying. Walking over to her, I pulled her into my chest.

"Baby, stop crying."

As soon as I said that, she cried harder, and my heart broke. I hated to see her cry. All of these years and I only made her cry once or twice, but that was when we were younger.

"Am I a bad mother? Am I ungrateful for everything you do for me? I know I complain a lot, but I am grateful for everything you do for me," she said once she calmed down.

"Why the fuck are you asking me that?"

She looked down, and I lifted her head. "Jade, you are an amazing mother. I would never be able to do half of the shit you do. Plus, you're doing it while obtaining your doctorate degree and working. You're like a superwoman. I couldn't ask for a better mother for my children. Even if you were ungrateful, I wouldn't care. Since I met you, I changed for the better to be able to take care of you. If it weren't for you, I wouldn't be able to afford a big ass house like this or spend the amount I am for our dream wedding. I was a young nigga with a decent amount of money, but you were the one who told me to go back to school and invest. That's what I did, and that's why I have everything I do now. Don't ever question yourself when it comes to being a mother or my wife. I love you to death." I kissed her on the cheek.

Forcing a smile, she wiped away her tears. "Thanks, baby. I love you too."

"What happened?" I asked her.

"I was on the phone with Kiya talking about both of our trips, then the couple's weekend and photoshoot in Aspen. Your mother told me I was using you because I didn't need a huge wedding, and that I was ungrateful. Oh, and that I'm a bad mom because she always has kids. After all, I'm always at the gym."

"I'll talk with her but in the meantime, you need to try finding people to help with the kids and clean up whenever you can't. That's my mother, but you and my children are more important to me. Your happiness comes before anyone. She needs to stop counting my pockets too. I don't need you stressing yourself out in front of the kids. I'll be staying home more too. My mother can move into my old apartment, so we can have the house back to ourselves," I told her.

After making sure she was straight, I told her to go check on the kids. Jade was stressed out, and I hated that my mother was the cause of it. I needed to talk with her. I should have put her in her place, but I was trying to keep the peace since we just got back on speaking terms. Jade was my heart and if that meant my mother had to go back to being a stranger, so be it. Looking around the bathroom, I found the lavender bubble bath and Epsom salt, so I ran her Jade a bath. Once that was finished, I lit the candles that were strategically placed around the room. I left out to get a bottle of wine and a glass. While she took a bubble bath, I was going to take care of the kids tonight.

"Jade, come here!" I yelled.

She hated when I yelled her name, so I knew she was about to say something smart.

"Why the hell are-- oh my!" she said when she saw I ran a bath for her.

"Take your clothes off and relax. I got the kids tonight."

I watched as she undressed. She filled out a little more once she got older and had kids. I loved her body the way it was; it didn't matter if she worked out or not. Her thighs were thicker and so was her ass. The extra weight looked good on her.

"Thank you, baby. I needed this."

"No problem, my love. I'll be back to check on you in a few."

The kids were still in bed when I walked back into our room. I picked up Callie while Cam followed behind me. We took the elevator downstairs. Jade didn't cook, so I googled restaurants to see what we were going to eat for dinner. I wasn't the best cook, and Jade didn't like for me to try. I settled on an Italian restaurant. Cam liked spaghetti and meatballs, so I ordered that for him. I wanted steak, shrimp scampi, and a baked potato. Jade was on a low carb diet, so I struggled with her order. I remembered her ordering chicken piccata and pasta. Since she couldn't have the noodles, I swapped them for zucchini noodles.

"Dang, fat mama, you can't even eat none of it," I said, tickling Callie.

While we waited for the food, we sat in the living room and watched Disney Plus. Cameron loved watching *Puppy Dog Pals*. He was into the show and sat on the floor, not moving with his eyes glued to the TV. Cam was bad, so I enjoyed him behaving. Callie was a daddy's girl all the way, so she sat on my lap. This was the best; sitting in the house with my kids. *Damn, I got kids.* Cameron was a spitting image of me except for his green eyes. Everything was me from his complexion to his facial features. He even had my toes. Callie was a mixture of me and her mother. I loved that she had Jade's chinky eyes, so you could tell they were Chinese. Like her brother, she inherited Jade's green eyes. She was the same complexion as her mother and had jet black curly hair. Cam and Callie were my pride and joy. God willing, I would be able to have more. I often thought about what if Jade never lost the first one. We would have had a six-year-old. Since I found out about her pregnancy, guilt consumed me. If it wasn't for me keeping Ronnie's pregnancy a secret, Jade would have never lost the baby or left me. Zeek was right. I needed to tell Jade, and soon. The doorbell interrupted my thoughts. It was the food.

Cam was in his highchair eating, so I took that as an opportunity to feed Callie. When he was finished, we went upstairs, and I bathed them together. Callie laid on the bed in her towel while I dressed Cam. After that, we walked to Callie's room, so she could get dressed. She was tired. I rocked her for five minutes, and she passed out.

"Let's go find a book to read," I said to Cam.

We laid in his bed reading a book about space. He loved books. Jade started reading to him once he was able to sit up on his own. She was an amazing mother. I don't know why my mother said differently. Jade thought she could do it all like her mother and not hire any help, but she needed it. What she didn't realize was that her mother only had one child, and we have two under the age of two. Between school, work, and taking care of everything else, she was beat. If she didn't take finding a nanny serious, I would. Jade was working part-time from home and on summer break from school, but that was going to end in a few more weeks, so she needed to get it together.

Cam went to sleep. I tried to ease off the bed without waking him. When I got to our room, Jade was sleeping. Smiling, I covered her up. She must have been exhausted. It was time to take my shower, so I could cuddle with my soon to be wife.

***

I sat in my old apartment waiting for my mother. Jade's been telling me about my mother saying slick shit, but I paid no attention to it. Seeing her cry made me feel like shit.

"Why are we here?" she asked, looking around.

"This is your new apartment. The rent is paid for a year and when the lease is up, you can let me know if you want to stay, so I can pay it for another year."

"I knew she was going to run to you like she always does." She rolled her eyes.

"What's your problem with her?"

"Nothing, she's too spoiled. The world doesn't revolve around her," she said, sounding jealous as fuck.

"My world revolves around her. She was spoiled before she got with me, and I plan on keeping it that way. If you don't respect her then I don't need you coming to the house. You're more than welcome to visit me and the kids, but you need to check that attitude at the door. If I had to choose, my pick would always be Jade and my family."

"So, you would stop talking to me for a female?" she questioned.

"For my wife, yes, I will. Just like you put all those men before me, I'm doing the same. It's no hard feelings, but I need to put my family first."

When my father left her, she looked for love in many different men instead of taking care of me. I was forced to sell drugs to to get the things I needed. Even though she didn't give a fuck about me, I made sure to give her money for her bills and to put food in her house. My grandmother begged me to forgive her so she could be in her grandchildren's life, and I agreed. She seemed to be doing good and I was happy everyone was getting along. If she didn't get her shit together, she wouldn't even be allowed to the wedding. Whatever Jade said went; I had no choice but to follow her lead.

"I will keep my thoughts to myself. Whenever you're home, I will come by to see the children."

"Ma, I want you to come over whether I'm there or not. You and Jade need to sit down and talk. That will be your daughter-in-law. She is a nice person. I know you think she's spoiled, but it's more to her. Do you see the jewelry I have on? Well, she got it for me. Her parents are rich, and Jade has her own money. She doesn't need mines. That's the reason I chose to marry her. She was the only female who wasn't impressed by material things," I explained.

"I'll take her out for lunch and apologize for my actions," she replied.

I left the apartment because I had to hit up the mall. The guys and I were leaving for Mexico in a few days.

Chapter Three

Jade

Kiya and I were doing last-minute running around for our girl's trip to Bali. I lost most of my pregnancy weight and my stomach went down significantly thanks to my diet, exercising, and my cavitation lipo treatment that tightened up my loose belly skin. I was bikini ready. We both needed a few more bathing suits. I had designer ones, but I needed something cheaper for some of the excursions we were going on. Heem's store had a few cute items I wanted to try on. It was the middle of October, and we wanted to do our separate trips before November. When we got back, it was going to be a little more than a month left, and we had another trip to take before Thanksgiving.

Dinner was going to be at our house this year. The menu was set so all I had to do was order my groceries because I was not stepping foot in the store around that time. Between last-minute food shopping and buying Christmas gifts, I was not willing to be around a bunch of people with Miss Rona going around. Everybody was still partying in large crowds with no masks on. My life was important to me and so was my children. The only way I agreed to go on this trip was for both groups to charter a private jet. We didn't have to step foot in an airport. Thank God I was marrying a man who could afford to do something like that. My bank account was nice, but I didn't have as much as Nasir. We both had separate accounts and one joint account. Our joint account paid for the bills and anything we needed for the family. My money was put up, so I could open my practice when I graduated.

"Let's stop to get something to eat before we leave," Kiya said to me.

"I can go for some Japanese food."

"Same girl. I haven't had any in such a long time."

It was a nice, warm day out, so we changed our minds and sat outside of the Cheesecake Factory to eat. I loved their lemonade. Plus, I wanted to take a nice hot shower and snuggle in my bed, eating a piece of cheesecake while binge-watching *The Golden Girls*. We ordered and waited for our food. I ordered something healthy because I was going to break my diet while on the trip, then it was back to eating healthy.

"How has the treatment been going?" I asked her.

"I hate it so much, Jade. The medication is making me a mean bitch. Heem could make dinner, rub my feet, take care of the baby, and I will still chew his head off. He's gon' divorce me, best friend," she pouted.

"Heem will not leave you. But you need to do this. It will be worth it when you're holding your baby."

"I know Fertile Myrtle, but I'm tired of all those shots and eating healthy all of the time."

"Tuhh, tell me about it. Nasir wants more kids. I am done for a while."

"After this one, I'm finished. I can't take this anymore. Has Nasir talked to his mother yet?" she asked, changing the subject.

"Girl, yes. She moved out and hasn't said anything to me since then. She'll stop by to see Nas and the kids but leave after an hour or so. I don't know what he said to her ass, but I'm happy as hell. She can stay wherever she's at."

"Excuse me, I have to use the bathroom," she excused herself.

Scrolling through my phone, I looked through social media to see if any of the guys posted pictures. Someone sat down, so I closed out of Instagram.

"That was quick."

"What's good, Jade," Donovan said.

Rolling my eyes, I huffed. "What do you want?" I asked him.

"I just wanted to say thank you for not bad mouthing me to Jill."

"You're welcome, but you should get going."

"What's the rush? I wanted to ask you something. Did Jill ever mention anything about getting married? When we first met, she said she never wanted to get married, but I think I'm ready to settle down. I don't want to ask her to marry me in front of everyone, and she says no."

"Oh my God! Yes, she wants to get married. That's all she talks about, but when you do it, propose in private," I told him.

Donovan walked away just as Kiya came back from the restroom. I was happy she didn't come back sooner.

"I know that wasn't Donovan's ass sitting here?" she asked.

"Yeah, he came over here to thank me for not bad-mouthing him to Jill. And he's about to propose to her."

"Wow! Dog ass Donovan is about to settle down. Never did I think he was the marrying type." She shrugged.

"I wouldn't marry his ass, but I'm not going to throw salt on someone else. Hopefully, he's a changed man because Jill is my girl."

After we ate and talked about what we wanted to do once we landed, we were ready to go home and finish packing up. Kiya paid for both of our lunches, and we headed to the car. While we were walking, someone caught my attention. This bitch was about to get the beating of a lifetime. I didn't forget how she put me and my unborn child's life in danger.

"Isn't that Dior over there?" Kiya asked.

"It sure is. Hold my bags while I beat her ass."

I practically ran over to her car, ready to beat the shit out of her. Dior's ass made sure to lay low this past year. Nasir told me to leave it alone, but this was something that needed to be done. Me and Cam would be dead right now. Mia died for some disrespectful shit, and I think Dior needed the same treatment. Nasir's ass has gotten soft since we had kids. The once ruthless bad boy who murdered people was long gone. A family man replaced him. He was going to be one of those fathers who wore a feather boa and crown while having tea with Callie when she got older. I didn't mind that, but I hated Dior so much that I had dreams of killing her ass. Nasir was that nigga and Lord knows I couldn't get him out of my system, but I would never endanger a pregnant woman for him. I cut my losses and walk away when a man shows me that he doesn't want me. To make matters worse, Nas didn't even leave her ass. He was still going to be with her if she knew how to be a team player. I mean, not for long because I would have eventually wanted my man back, and Nasir wasn't saying no to me or his son.

Before we got to her car, she closed the door and held a baby in her arms. He was a cute, light-skinned baby with the same curly hair as my son. He looked to be a little younger than Cameron. I stopped in my tracks to study the little boy's features.

Looking for signs of Nasir, I stood there. Kiya grabbed my arm and pulled me away.

"I know what you're thinking. Stop it now!" she said to me.

"Dior's ass is darker than you with that light ass baby. He has the same complexion and curly hair as Cameron. Kiya, if you saw a bitch Heem used to fuck with and she had a baby that sort of resembled him, you would be feeling the same way." I looked at her.

"It does look suspicious, but like you told me last year, wait and speak to your fiancé. Do not stress yourself out over nothing."

"Fine!" I huffed.

***

I sat on my bed scrolling through Dior's Facebook page. Her son was so handsome. She never posted any pictures of her baby father. I didn't want to believe Nasir fathered a child that wasn't with me. Maybe that's the reason he wanted to leave her alone. She was the mother of his child. I needed to talk to him, but his service was acting weird in Mexico. If the trip wasn't paid for, I would cancel it and head to Mexico to find his ass. I prayed I was overreacting. There was no way I could deal with Dior for the rest of my life. Nasir has been great this past year. Maybe I needed to stop thinking about it and wait till he comes home. The trip was expensive, so I needed to get my mind right.

***

Our private jet landed at Ngurah Rai International Airport. When I stepped off, I couldn't believe my view. I've been to nice places before, but this was something different. I couldn't wait to go exploring. I wanted to wear something simple on my first night. The flight was long as hell, and I wanted to be comfortable. The cream Maxi dress covered my Chanel espadrilles, my hair was in a topknot, and the only makeup I wore was nude lip gloss. Nasir rented two trucks to chauffer us around on our trip.

We pulled up to the Villa, and my mouth dropped. The 12055 square feet villa was breathtaking. There were 4 bedrooms, 5 bathrooms, and we had an amazing few of the ocean. I couldn't wait to have a lazy day by the beach. It also came with a family room, two pools, a patio, movie theater, sauna, and gym. We got out of the trucks and made our way inside. Someone was waiting there with drinks in their hand. I grabbed one and took a sip.

"Keep these shits coming," Crystal sang.

"Here we go," I laughed.

"Don't start," Kiya said to both of us.

Walking to the backyard, I was in awe. There was a pond with fish near the fire pit. We went to check the rest of the house out. When I got home, I was going to talk to Nasir. We needed to invest in a vacation home here. Maybe he could go in with Heem and Zeek. All I know is I wanted to come here more often. We all went to our rooms to shower and take a quick nap.

Later that night, we sat outside waiting for our dinner. The fire pit was lit as well as torches around the yard. Music played softly in the background. Since it was my first time in Bali, I wanted to try some of their food. I could have Americanized food back home. Tonight, I wanted to try something new. Crystal wasn't used to shit like this, so we had rice and chicken for her if she didn't want to have what we were eating. While we waited, we talked about their dresses. I would be wearing a satin ivory gown with long sleeves. I wanted a very simple dress that would be timeless since I was saving it for Callie. Kiya was my matron of honor so she was going to wear a gold sequin dress while the other girls wore a burgundy dress. The men all were going to wear black pants with suede burgundy jackets. Nasir was going to be in all black minus his ivory tie. I couldn't wait to see how everyone looked.

"Before we start eating, I just want to make a toast," Kiya said, standing up. "Jade, words can't express how happy I am for you. The moment you laid eyes on my brother in front of the Klein Memorial, I knew you liked him. I say it was love at first sight even though y'all couldn't stand each other. I'm so happy, I got to witness you two fall in love and bring two beautiful children into this world. I love that he makes you happy and treats you like the queen you are. Eight years later, and you two are going to be husband and wife. Congratulations!" Kiya said, wiping the tears from her eyes.

We wiped our tears, and I stood up to hug her. "Thank you! You know how much of a journey this has been, and I can't wait to end this year as Jade Nami Miller."

"Damn, y'all getting married. I never thought it would happen, but I'm happy for you, Jade. I know sometimes we bump heads and I say slick shit about him, but I'm blessed to witness how much he loves you. Congratulations, Jade," Crystal said, pulling me into a hug.

"Thank you so much. I really appreciate that, Crys."

The dinner was bomb, and we enjoyed the conversation we were having. Crystal was telling us about this guy she's been dating. It was getting pretty serious between the two. I told her to bring him to the wedding, so I could meet him. We called it a night early because first thing in the morning, we were going to see animals at the Zoo then walk through the Sacred Monkey Forest Sanctuary.

***

"Look at that tiger cub," Kiya gushed. "Let's go pet it."

Walking over to the zookeeper, we asked to take a picture. One by one, we sat and played with the baby tigers. They were so cute but a little feisty. I had to keep my fingers away because they kept nipping at it. The next thing we went to see were the lions and other big cats. I wanted to chill on an elephant's back and take a picture. After staying there for a few hours, we went to the forest to chill with the monkeys. Crystal didn't want to go, but we dragged her.

"I'm telling y'all now, if one of these fuckers touch me, it's going to be a problem." Crystal rolled her eyes.

"Stop being so scared all the time. All we're doing is walking through the forest," Kiya said to her.

We got out, and I'd never experienced something like this. There were monkeys all over. At first, I was hesitant, but they weren't worried about anything we were doing. Taking my phone out, I started recording videos and taking pictures. When I got home, I planned on making a scrapbook for this trip. The further we walked, the more monkeys there were. Crystal stopped to take a picture, but a monkey came up to her, snatched her phone and ran away.

"I told y'all I wasn't fucking with these stupid ass monkeys. They're stealing my shit like we back in Bridgeport!" she yelled, chasing after the mischievous creature.

Kiya, Ava, and I stood there laughing at her talking shit and chasing the monkey. I took my phone out and started recording.

"I got something for your little ass!" Crystal screamed.

Putting my phone away, I had some nuts in my bag, so I took it out and shook it. The monkey who had her phone stopped and came over to me. I snatched the phone, and we ran to the truck. I didn't need them shits taking anything from me.

"My stomach hurts so much from laughing," Ava laughed.

"I got the whole shit recorded too. Crystal was mad as hell,"

I told them.

"Send that shit to my phone, now!" Kiya chuckled.

"Fuck yall!" Crystal shouted.

We got back to the house and changed into our bathing suits. I had a pink Fendi print one-piece bathing suit with the side cut out from the Nicki Minaj collection that I've wanted to wear for the longest. We were going to chill on the beach and watch the sunset. After such an eventful day, I wanted to relax. Walking down to the beach, we found a few chairs and put our bags down.

"Omg, look at the elephants walking toward us." Ava pointed.

When I turned around, two guys were walking with elephants our way. I smiled because they stopped in front of us.

"This is for Jade," the shorter guy said, holding an envelope.

Grabbing it, I opened it and read what was inside. I wanted to cry at how thoughtful my future husband was.

Jade,

You couldn't stop talking about riding elephants on the beach. With this whole COVID thing going on, those rides were canceled. You're my world and I love making you smile, so I brought the elephants to you. Enjoy your ride in the sunset. Make sure to take pictures and send them to me.

Nas

"What does it say, Jade?" Kiya snatched the letter from me. "Awww, this is so sweet."

"I love that man," I smiled.

After talking to the men, we all were helped on the backs of the elephants. They played in the ocean while we held on for dear life. The water was deep enough, so I jumped off its back into the water. We chilled on the beach for about two hours before we decided to get dinner.

It was the last night of our trip and we were getting ready to head to dinner at a popular restaurant Salon Bali. The reviews were amazing, and I couldn't wait to try the food. I sat on the bed in nothing but a towel while trying to get in contact with Nasir. Besides a few texts here and there, we haven't kept in contact. I was in Bali, and he was in Mexico. I was having the time of my life, but my mind kept drifting to Dior and her baby.

"We're ready… Girl, why aren't you dressed? Please don't tell me you're still thinking about Dior. Nasir wouldn't keep something like that from you," Kiya stressed.

"I can't help it but let me put my clothes on so we can enjoy our last night here. We're definitely getting white girl wasted tonight." I smiled.

Putting all the negative thoughts in the back of my mind, I got up so we could head out.

Chapter Four

Nasir

I tried to keep my mind off of the stressful situation I had back home. Mexico was fun as hell, and I wanted to come back with Jade. She liked to immerse herself in different cultures. That was my baby, and I couldn't wait to get home to her. I missed the hell out of my kids too.

"I bet you he's over there thinking about Jade," Heem laughed.

"You know he is. This nigga better hurry up before I change my damn mind!" Zeek yelled.

We were about to go zip-lining through the jungle. It was up high, and I was getting nervous. Heem was always ready to do shit like this.

"Yo'! You sure this shit isn't going to break on me?" I asked the instructor.

"It's safe," he replied.

I side-eyed him. The reviews on the place we came to were good enough, but I was still hesitant. If the rope were to break, I would be paralyzed or even dead.

"Don't chicken out now," Zeek smirked.

"Ain't nobody scared, I lied.

Heem went first and he seemed to enjoy it, so I was down for whatever at this point. The attendant strapped me to everything, and I was ready to go. Looking down, I said a quick prayer and let go. The wind hit my face, and I admired zipping through the trees. Monkeys were as high as I was. A chilling sound could be heard and when I looked to my right, I could see a Jaguar running underneath me. My mouth hung open; I couldn't believe what I was seeing. A predator was so close to me but still so far. I prayed that shit didn't follow me to where I was landing. A minute later, I could see where Heem was standing waiting for us, but the big cat was nowhere in sight.

"Nahhh, I ain't never doing any shit like that again. We are going back to the resort ASAP! Did you see that fucking jaguar running?" I said as soon as I landed.

"What are you talking about?" He eyed me.

I explained to him what I saw while it was my turn, and he couldn't believe it. Shit like that only happened in a movie or something.

"Take my ass back to the resort. I am done with this exploring shit! First, we see a damn shark while scuba diving, now a fucking lion about to eat us!" Zeek shouted.

We both laughed at how dramatic he was being. "That's not a fucking lion, Zeek," I chuckled.

"I don't care what it is. It has teeth and can eat me, so I'm out. I'm trying to make it back home to my wife and son."

"Don't worry, I already said I had enough of this wild shit today. Let's go get ready for dinner."

There were two days left on our trip, and we had a big

dinner planned. Heem also mentioned something about throwing my bachelor party here instead of in the states. When we got back, we had another trip to Aspen, Thanksgiving then our wedding and Christmas. It was going to be a busy few months.

***

After dinner, Heem drove us to some bar that was in the desert. It looked like the shit in that movie *From Dusk Till Dawn* where everybody in the club turned into vampires. Come to think about it, it took place in Mexico too. See, this nigga Heem always had to be different. Instead of hiring dancers to come to the hotel, he had us out in the middle of nowhere. We were strapped up but still. The three of us weren't a match for the Cartel if they wanted to come get us.

"I'm not going on vacation with y'all niggas again. What type of usk till dawn bar you got us going to?" Zeek asked Heem.

"Yo' that's crazy, I was just thinking of that movie. We could have had some dancers come to the room or something."

"Y'all niggas mad annoying. Shut the fuck up." Heem laughed.

Walking inside, I was surprised by how the inside looked. It was modern and the dancers were bad as hell. One of them looked like that Mexican singer Selena. She winked at me.

"I think we should have done something else. You know Nas got a thing for strippers. I don't need Jade trying to beat my ass," Zeek said to us.

"You're right. Maybe we should chill by the bar at the resort."

"That was the old Nas. I'll be a married man soon. Ain't nothing a bitch can do for me," I replied.

"Yeah, okay. Better be on your best behavior or I'm calling

Jade."

The music was okay, but it wasn't anything I would have listened to if I were alone. They worried about me messing with a stripper, but these females weren't my type. They had nice shapes but not enough ass for my liking. I honestly was ready to go home and be with my family. This strip club was so different from the ones in the states. Everybody would be making it rain, but this was new. The dancers had their money tucked in their outfits or in a satin bag. Our section was full of dancers, and we tipped them well. I was over it. There was important shit that needed to be handled back home. The Selena look-alike made her way over to me and danced on my lap. She looked even better up close and smelled like vanilla.

"You want to go to a private room?" she whispered.

"I'm fine right where I'm at," I replied.

I wasn't about to get caught up with no female that wasn't Jade. Plus, I wasn't trying to go somewhere alone with her, then she lie and say I did something to her. Nobody knew where we were, so I was playing it smart.

"It's your night, go enjoy yourself." Zeek laughed.

"Hell no! Shorty can dance with me right here. Jade's ass wouldn't like another woman on me anyways."

"I didn't know Jade had you scared like this."

"I'm not scared of her, but I respect her," I replied.

Three hours later, we staggered out of the bar. I didn't mean to get fucked up, but the tequila was so good. All three of us kept taking shots. We had to call a taxi to get back to the resort because none of us were sober enough to drive.

"You know I got you, bro." Heem wrapped his arm around my neck. "I'm happy you finally found a woman to spend the rest of your life with."

Every time we got drunk, Heem liked to get all emotional. I couldn't wait till I got back to the resort, so I could go my separate way. The whole car ride he kept telling me how proud he was of me. Zeek's ass was sleeping with his head against the window. And his ass was snoring. I knew this was my last time going out with them. Once we got back to the resort, my drunk ass had to help them to their rooms before I made it to mine. Soon as I walked into my room, I plopped down on the couch and went to sleep.

The next morning, the sun was bright and woke me out of my drunken slumber. Walking to the bathroom, I took a long piss and hopped in the shower. After brushing my teeth, I looked at my phone. There were ten missed calls from Jade. When I called her back, I couldn't get thru. We hadn't spoken to each other in a few days. Being in different time zones made it hard to keep in contact. I left it alone because I was heading to the states soon.

***

I sat in the Doctor's office nervous as hell. How could this be happening to me? I was young, not even thirty. I had two amazing children at home, a fiancée who adored me, and a life most people would kill for. It was like I could hear the clock ticking. My stomach was in knots. I wish Jade could be here with me, but her plane landed tomorrow.

"Good afternoon, Mr. Miller. I have your lab results today," Dr. Gupta said. "So, it looks like I was right. You have pancreatic cancer."

That was all I heard before I stopped focusing on his words. My children weren't even five yet, and there was a chance I was going to leave them. How was my baby going to handle this?

"Mr. Miller, are you okay? Did you hear anything I said?" he asked me.

"I spaced out for a minute. You can continue now."

"I know this is a lot to take in, but we did catch it early. When I say that, I mean very early. With this type of cancer, we don't catch it until it's too late because when someone has cancer in the pancreas, there are often no symptoms. A routine blood work, physical, and imaging may have saved your life. Since it's still early, I have high hopes of your chances of survival," he said.

I nodded my head to let him know I heard him.

"There are five stages of cancer. They range from zero to five, five being the worst. Now, you have stage zero. That means it has not spread and is only on the top layer of cells in the pancreas," he continued.

"So, what does that mean for me? What are the treatment options?" I asked him.

"I want to start chemotherapy for the time being. Then we can try surgery to get a look inside to make sure there are no tumors. It can be treated and, in your case, may even be curable. I'll have the nurse reach out to you so we can set chemo up. Don't stress yourself out," he said, before getting up.

I sat there trying to come up with a way to tell Jade without her overreacting. Maybe I needed to keep it to myself until I had surgery. Getting up, I walked to my car. A drink was well needed at this moment. After today, I was going to stop smoking, drinking, and watch what kind of food I put into my body. I remember reading about a certain type of diet that can help with cancer treatments. My mother sent me a text telling me to meet her for lunch. I told Jade's mother I would pick the kids up once I finished.

Shaking my head, I pulled up to Red Lobster. I didn't want to be here with her at this moment. All I wanted to do was get my kids and spend the rest of the night with them. She was waiting for me when I walked in. Once we were seated, I ordered a shot of whiskey.

"It's too early to be drinking, son," my mother said to me.

"I need it. What did you want to talk to me about?"

"Well… ummmm…" she stuttered.

"Just spit it out. I'm not trying to be here all day. Jade will be home tomorrow, so I need to make sure to put the kids to bed on time."

"You're always taking up for her." She rolled her eyes.

"That's going to be my wife soon, of course, I'm going to defend her!" I snapped.

"Well, while you were in Mexico, she was going out with other guys," she said, showing me the picture of Jade and her ex at a table.

They both were smiling, and I felt sick to my stomach. What could Jade possibly be doing with him? I couldn't wait until her ass got back to Connecticut. Not only did I have to deal with my diagnosis, I needed to figure out why she was out with an ex. Since we got back together, I haven't talked to Dior or Ashley, let alone go out to lunch with them. Jade would have a fit. But I guess she didn't have to follow her own rules.

"Did you say something to her?" I asked.

"Why would I? That's your girl and you were away. She doesn't like me like that. I told you all of those times she claimed to go to the gym she was doing something else. You don't need to marry that girl. Might as well call it quits."

"I have to ask Jade about the picture so send it to my phone. Thanks for letting me know," I said, getting up to leave.

My mother didn't like Jade for whatever reason, and I always took her side. Now, to have my mother see Jade out with someone was a slap in the face. I hated to defend someone and feel stupid in the process. There was too much shit on my mind to think about Jade fucking around on me. I was going to ask her to avoid any confusion.

Jade's mother told me she was going to keep the kids for the night. That gave me time to relax in the house alone. The five-star resort in Mexico couldn't compare to my house in the states. I ordered a salad for dinner. After my shower, I decided to get some sleep. I still had jet lag.

The next morning, the sound of the alarm woke me up. Grabbing my phone, I looked to see who was coming inside. It was Jade. I went to the bathroom, so I could brush my teeth before she came into the room. After waiting for over ten minutes, she never came upstairs. Walking down, I noticed her bags by the door, but she was gone. Shaking my head, I went to take a shower. Two hours later, she came in with the kids. A few seconds later, a group of people came in with boxes and a huge Christmas tree.

"Baby, take the kids upstairs while I manage these people!" she yelled at me.

"Damn, you just got back. I need to talk to you about something in private."

"We can go to our room and talk. I have about five minutes before I need to get back."

"Never mind." I grabbed the kids and headed upstairs.

Jade sent someone with food upstairs a few hours later. After the kids ate, I got them ready for bed. I was pissed she didn't have a full conversation with me when she first got here. Almost two weeks apart and she acts like she didn't miss me. Baseball was on and since I was alone, I went into my man cave to watch the game. Grabbing a beer, I turned on the TV and tuned in. I heard Jade calling my name, but I ignored her.

"You didn't hear me calling you?" she asked.

"Nope."

"Somebody is grumpy," she giggled.

Walking over to me, she sat on my lap and kissed me. "Thank you for my trip. I enjoyed myself, especially riding the elephants in the ocean. That meant a lot to me."

"You're welcome."

"I'm trying to talk to you and your attention is on the game!" she snapped.

"And I was trying to get your attention earlier. Leave me alone, I'm watching the game."

Her eyes got watery, and she stormed out. I immediately felt like shit and got up to chase after her. We've been on good terms and haven't argued since we got back together. When I went downstairs, I was in awe. Jade had the whole downstairs decorated. This year, she went very traditional. Red, green, and gold trees, wreaths, and other Christmas items decorated the house. It was my first time having my house decorated. Last Christmas, we only put a tree up since Cam was still a baby. I admit, I overreacted. We were a few days away from November which meant our wedding was getting closer. We couldn't wait to put our decorations up since we were leaving for Aspen in a few weeks. Then when we got back, from there it was going to be a few short weeks until the wedding. Our tuxedos were getting made in Paris, so we had to make sure they would be here on time. Especially with this whole COVID situation going on. Jade just had to have them custom made. Planning a wedding was stressful as hell. I thought all I had to do was get dressed and show up, but Jade wanted a lot. Just like our trip to Aspen. We were only going there to take our wedding pictures. I was going to ask her if we should invite more of our family and have Thanksgiving there, so we didn't have to rush back and have to prepare a huge meal.

Jade was in the kitchen throwing away some of the food that went bad. She looked at me and rolled her eyes at me.

"I'm sorry for treating you like that. Come give daddy a hug." I held my arms out.

"Nigga, please. You better be lucky I didn't punch you in the face."

"You're so violent," I laughed, trying to get her to smile.

"What do you want? I'm busy now."

"I can help you."

We cleaned the kitchen and told each other about our trips. My stomach hurt so much from laughing at the video of Crystal's ghetto ass chasing the monkey. I wanted to visit Bali now that she showed me all of the pictures and videos. Her phone started ringing. She looked at the number and walked away before she answered it. I followed her to see who she was talking to. She was in the laundry room, but I couldn't hear what she was saying. I walked away before she came out. Acting like I was doing something, she came back and finished up her story.

"Who was that?" I asked her.

"A friend."

"Which friend?"

"Nasir, why are you all in my business? I said a friend so leave it at that. What's with all these questions?"

"I asked you one question and you didn't tell me. It's like you're hiding something."

"Hmmm, then that makes two of us then." She rolled her eyes.

Before I could respond, the doorbell rang.

"I'll go get it." She walked away.

I never was the type to act this way, but Jade was up to something, and I was going to find out what it was. My mother showed me that picture, and I haven't been able to get it out of my mind. We needed to have a serious talk before she walked down that aisle.

Chapter Five

Kiya

Jade and Nasir were finally getting married. I was so happy for them. After all the drama they were finally getting it together. We pushed the Aspen trip back by almost two weeks so we could celebrate Thanksgiving here. The kids were with us and we hired two nannies to help watch them when we were out taking the wedding pictures. The house we rented was amazing. Although it was a cabin, it was very modern. There were 6 bedrooms, 7.5 baths, state of the art kitchen, game room, jacuzzi, karaoke bar, sauna, and gym. This was the perfect winter getaway. Every time I went on vacation, it was somewhere warm. This was different, and I liked it. I couldn't wait to go skiing for the first time. If Jade wasn't getting married on Christmas, I would have suggested we come here. Back in Connecticut, it barely snowed in December. I wanted the kids to be able to experience a white Christmas like I did as a child. If you ask me, I think it's climate change. It just started getting cold in the fall and winter months.

"This shit is nice as hell," Heem said to me.

"Watch your mouth in front of Heemie. You know he has a potty mouth," I scolded my husband.

"My bad, baby, but this is really nice. Jade is dramatic. This is our second trip for the wedding, and we still have a month to go."

"I know, I'm tired. I can't wait till all of this over. 2021 is going to be a good year. No more wedding plans and no more Trump. Happy as hell his ass is out of here after December," I said to him.

We gathered our bags and made our way inside. It was beautifully decorated with a Christmas theme except the dining room; it had fall decorations since we were having Thanksgiving here. Heemie ran around the house looking around. It was the first time he'd been out of Connecticut. By the time he was old enough to travel, COVID hit and we weren't able to take him anywhere. I mean, he could have gone somewhere if we rented a jet, but I didn't want to risk it since he was so young. Hopefully, this shit will end soon now that Trump is going to be out of office in January. If he would have acted responsibly then the shit wouldn't have gotten this bad. We wanted to take the kids to Disney World but ended up canceling the trip.

"Holy shit this is nice. I'm so glad y'all met Heem and Nasir because I've been getting to travel everywhere for free!" Crystal yelled as she walked in.

Walking to the entrance, I looked at her up and down. I don't know who paid for it, but she was dressed in a fox fur coat, Balmain high-rise jeans, a cashmere turtleneck, and Fendi boots. Now, my cousin could dress her ass off in a Macy's and Fashion Nova kind of way, but the bitch in front of me was giving me rich bitch vibes, and I loved it. Her hair, usually covered by a wig, was in a short cut and dyed blonde.

"Uh uh, bitch you talking about free trips, but that outfit is about eight stacks. Who got you in this drip?" I questioned.

Smiling, she replied. "I have a new boo."

"Bitch, let's get some wine and give me the tea."

Heem had the baby, so I could catch up with Crystal. Grabbing a bottle of Cheval-Blanc, I lit the fireplace and we sat down. It was just us for now. Jade and Nasir were going to be here in another hour or two. Zeek and Ava were flying in tomorrow with their son.

"So, tell me his name."

"His name is Rashad. He's a rapper from Bridgeport. We met at one of his shows almost a year ago. Kiya, he is so amazing. I think I'm in love," she beamed.

I knew exactly what Rashad she was talking about. There was a gay guy, Shaunie, that did me and Jade's hair at a salon downtown. His friend Aaliyah used to date the guy Rashad, and he was a dog. He'd gotten this ghetto chick pregnant twice and wasn't going to tell the girl. She ended up finding out anyway and caught a case. The whole shit was a bunch of drama. I remember hearing about how much of a hoe he was. My cousin was feeling him, and I didn't want to burst her bubble, so I kept it to myself. I was for sure about to ask a few questions though.

"Does he have kids?" I asked.

"Yes, he has two. We go out with them all of the time. They're too cute, but his baby mother is going to get her ass beat one of these days," she told me.

"Oh, so you guys are serious?"

"Very! He was talking about getting a place together, but I think it's too soon. I want to take it slow. In every relationship I've been in, I never took my time to get to know them, and I always end up hurt. I'm not getting any younger, Kiya. I'm around all of you and sometimes I feel left out. I'm the only one who isn't getting married or even engaged. I have a son I need to think about, and that means I need to get my shit together," she sighed.

"I understand what you're saying, but we met our men

when we were teenagers. That's why we have our shit together. It's been over five years. You know how toxic Jade and Nasir's relationship was, but they had history and made shit work. When you were younger, you wanted to be free and experience life. You did, so now it's the perfect time to start building something. Don't feel like you have to rush and get married because we are. Take your time to find the man of your dreams whether it's this Rashad guy or someone new."

"Thank you for that, Kiy. I just feel like I'm so behind in everything. Maybe I should have taken life more seriously. Rashad is cool, but I need to make sure he's serious about this relationship. I love that he spoils me, but I'm kind of tired of his baby mother. She is a miserable bitch. He was telling me about his ex-girlfriend Aaliyah, and I wish she was the one I had to deal with," she laughed.

"Yeah, Aaliyah is mad cool. We get our hair done at her friend's shop. Just keep your eyes on him because I heard how he did Aaliyah, and I will have him fucked up if he tries that shit with you," I chuckled.

"What y'all heifers in here talking about?" Nasir said.

"Boy, if you don't shut up. They put *Girlfriends* on Netflix and his ass binged watched it with me, now he thinks he's William," Jade explained.

"Ain't nobody worried about what Nasir was talking about," I said to them.

"Get the bags," she told him and walked away.

The way she said it let me know something was up with them. I needed to get the guys out of the house, so we could all catch up. I would have suggested we go somewhere, but I needed to be in a nice, warm house. The cold wasn't my thing, but I was taking my ass skiing tomorrow.

"Hey, Heem, do you think you can run and grab a few things for me?" I asked.

"Sure. Nasir, take this ride with me."

They put all the bags in the room and left. Both Calli and Cam were sleeping, so she used that as an opportunity to start unpacking. I watched her move around the room, slamming drawers in the process. Her mood was off. This wasn't the happy Jade that was in Bali a few weeks ago. Crystal was on the phone with her man and our sons were in the game room playing.

"What's wrong with you?" I asked her.

"Girl, everything. Since I got back home, shit hasn't been the same. The whole thing with Dior is still on my mind. He's been disappearing for hours at a time and then comes home and tells me a lie each time. Where is he spending his time?"

"I thought you were going to ask him about it? Why are you still walking around here with that shit on your mind?"

"Easier said than done. We both know all he does is lie. He lied about Mia, then the bitch who was putting glitter on him and Ronnie. I wouldn't even believe his ass. I was going to ask him, but then he started questioning me about who was calling or texting me. And every time I go to the gym, he bugs out. I'm so annoyed, Kiya."

"Damn! You two are about to get married in a month. It's the holidays and y'all aren't getting along. If you need us to keep the kids while you two go out to eat and talk, I can do that. Now is not the time to be arguing," I lectured.

"I know, Kiya. We were doing fine until I got back from Bali. I don't know what happened since then. The vibes are all off."

"Jade, I'm not playing, you need to talk to him. Anyways, the kitchen is stocked with everything we need to cook for dinner."

"We're not hiring someone to cook?" she asked me.

"No, bitch. We are cooking our meal, so you better get it together. It will be fun. You can just make desserts or something."

"That's okay then. I wasn't trying to be in here on no family holiday movie type of shit. I just came to take these pictures and relax," she laughed.

"Girl bye." I threw the throw pillow at her.

"All I know is we're ordering out tonight. Driving here with two kids tired my ass out. I think their asses are out for the night. They already have their PJs on, so I'm not even waking them up. Cam bad as hell!"

"Yea, he is, Jade. I don't know how you do it," I said before walking away.

***

I sent Heem out over an hour ago, and they still weren't back. We all ate and were in the bed. I wanted to get up and make a nice breakfast before we all went skiing, so I was about to call it a night. My son was sleeping, and I was about to do the same.

The next morning, Heem was in the bed, passed out, snoring. I shook my head and got up to take a shower. The house was quiet which meant everyone was probably still sleeping. I was always the first one up anyways. After washing my body a few times with my soap from Peace of Love Beauty Bars, I rinsed off and got out. Once my morning hygiene was complete, I threw on my Skims velour sweatsuit and Ugg slippers.

When I got to the kitchen, there were bottles of liquor all over the counter. That's why Heem's ass came to bed so late. Him and Nasir were up drinking all night. It was cool though because if his ass wasn't up when it was time to go skiing, I was leaving him. Going into the fridge, I pulled out eggs, bacon, sausage, milk, butter, and an array of fruits. Then I walked to the pantry and got everything I needed to make my homemade pancakes and waffles. Jade and the kids came down 30-minutes later as I was finishing the last of the pancakes. Heemie was with her. She put all the kids in their highchairs and helped me serve the food. Crystal and her son came down soon after.

"It smells so good, Kiya. I am starving!" Jade said, rubbing her stomach.

"It sure does. You know this bitch is the black Martha Stewart," Crystal laughed.

"I was thinking more of Julia Child," Jade snickered.

"Aht, aht! Just because y'all bitches barely cook doesn't mean I go overboard," I told them.

"I cook all the time, but you prepare mad food. Does Heem even eat every time you cook? He is still kind of skinny, so I know his ass is not eating," Jade replied.

"Don't touch the food then." I rolled my eyes.

"I mean, I'ma still eat it but damn," Crystal said.

"Both of y'all can just be quiet. Pick whatever you want to eat. I'm going to wake Heem's ass up. Him and Nas were up late as hell drinking."

"I bet they were." Jade rolled her eyes.

***

The nannies were in the lodge with the kids. They had their ski training, but it was too cold to have them out. Jade and I were on the ski lift heading to the top of the mountain. The guys were already at the top. They met us here an hour ago and were snowboarding. I guess they did this shit before. All I wanted to do was get a few cute pictures for the gram and take my ass back in the house. I hated the cold weather.

"Are you coming to the hot springs with us later?" Jade asked me.

"Yes, I'm excited about that, but I'm going to the cabin after this. It's too cold for me."

"Well, I'm coming with you. It's freezing. This Chanel snowsuit is cute, but I'm ready to take it off."

Once we got to the top, I looked down and my stomach was in knots. I always did this when I was at the top but going down wasn't that bad. I made my way over to where I needed to be and almost bust my ass in the process.

"Oh, hell no, Jade. I can't believe you got me doing this shit!" I yelled over to her.

"It's kind of fun. Let's go on the count of three." She laughed. "One, two, three."

I pushed myself forward and the air hit my face. She was right, it was kind of fun, but I would never get used to this. Aspen was nice, but I couldn't see myself coming back. The problem with Jade is that she watches the Kardashians and wants to do the shit they are doing. As I was nearing the bottom of the mountain, someone in the way, so I tried to go around them and ended up running into Jade. We both tried to catch ourselves, but I ended up falling on top of her.

"See, I told your ass. Get up so we can get out of here."

Skiing wasn't that bad, but I was happy I got to experience it with Jade and the kids. The guys were on some extreme sports shit, and I wasn't with all of that. We gathered the kids and went back to the house. I had a one-piece bathing suit with long sleeves. Even though the water in the spring was hot, it was still freezing outside, and I wanted to be covered up.

"How was it? I would have gone, but I don't do those white people activities," Crystal said.

"I bet you're dead serious too." I shook my head.

Jade was in the corner snickering. Crystal always said some out-of-pocket shit. I didn't have time to entertain them. Grabbing my son, I went upstairs to get him ready for his nap, and I was going to take one too. When I woke up, it was dark outside. I looked over and Heemie wasn't in the bed.

"He's with the nanny in the game room," Heem said, coming out of the shower.

I was still in love with my husband, but I was ready to give up on trying to have another baby. I couldn't find the right words to tell him I didn't want to continue with the treatment. All he ever talked about was having a house full of kids, and I didn't think that was going to happen. The hormones were having a negative effect on my body.

"Heem, we need to talk," I said to him.

"Uh oh. What did you do now?" he questioned.

"Me? Boy, hush and come here. I know we both wanted more kids, but I can't keep up this process. We can look into some other options like surrogacy or adoption," I explained.

"I kind of figured that. It's okay, Kiya, so don't go blaming yourself. Let's get through this wedding and the holidays, and we can talk about it after the New Year." He kissed me on the lips.

"Are you sure?" I asked him.

"I'm positive. You and Junior are all I need. If God blesses us with another child in the future, I'll be grateful, but I have my family now. Don't get back into that place you were a couple of years ago. I love and married you, not your womb," he chuckled.

"I love you too. Thank you for reassuring me. You know how I get when I'm overthinking."

Knock! Knock! Knock!

"Come in!" I yelled.

"We are leaving in twenty-minutes," Jade said to me.

***

The hot water felt amazing on my skin. After a long morning of skiing and falling, I was able to relax. I was sitting on Heem's lap with my head against his chest.

"This is why I should have told my boo to come. I hate that I'm the third wheel. Zeek and Ava even showing PDA, and I've never even seen them hug before., Crystal pouted.

"You should have talked to Jade about it. I would have loved to officially meet him," I said to her.

"Who?" Heem asked.

"She messes with that rapper Rashad from Bridgeport," I replied.

"The one with the braids? Damn, Crystal, you should have told him to come. Invite his ass to the wedding."

"He's coming because I refuse to be lonely at a wedding."

"She takes forever like we are going out to dinner or something," Nas sighed, getting into the water.

"Why wasn't her bathing suit under her clothes?" I asked, confused. "Oh, never mind, I see why," I snickered.

Just like I said, Jade's ass thinks her last name is Kardashian. She stood in front of us in the same fur bikini and boots as Kim K.

Nasir shook his head and helped her while she took off her boots. Since Jade had gotten back, we both were preoccupied. I don't remember her ass being this extra. The outfit was cute but not needed. Were you even supposed to get fur wet? I mean, I guess because animals bathe.

"This is why your ass took forever? Too busy back there killing a Mink for its fur," Nasir said to her, making us all laugh.

"Nope, a few guys tried to talk to me. That's what took me forever." She rolled her eyes.

I could see the vein in his neck throbbing and before he could say something, I tried to change the subject to avoid an argument.

"Are you guys ready to take our pictures?" I asked.

"Hell yes, so I can get my ass back home. Jade is lucky I love her because it's cold as hell out here," Ava replied.

"Yes, girl, and my boo waiting for me back home," Crystal said.

We stayed in the hot springs for a while before we decided to call it a night. We all had to get up early, so we could get our makeup and hair done. Back at the house, Jade was watching a movie with all of the kids. The guys were in the game room playing the new Xbox. I needed some quiet time, so I was off to the side reading a book with a nice cup of tea. Nasir walked over and scrolled through his phone. His whole demeanor was off while he looked at whatever he was reading. I didn't want to think Jade was right, but something was up with him.

"What are you doing?" I asked.

"Oh shit, you scared me." He jumped.

"What's going on with you and Jade?"

"I don't know. Shit's been different since we got back from our trips. And when I try to talk to her, she gets an attitude or tries to act busy. We're getting married in a month and it's like we're drifting apart," he sighed.

"I can tell you right now why that's happening. Both of y'all are keeping secrets. I've been telling Jade that both of you need to sit down and talk about whatever is bothering y'all. Look at the shit me and Heem went through. It all could have been avoided if we sat down and talked it out. Learn from our mistakes. Since 2012 I've wanted y'all together and y'all are almost there. A month is closer than y'all think," I lectured.

"I'll go talk to her now," he replied, getting up.

I prayed they talked and worked everything out. It's been a long time coming, and we all were holding our breath, waiting for them to make it official.

Chapter Six

Jade

I smiled looking at my bridesmaids. They all looked beautiful, especially Kiya. They wore burgundy off the shoulder dresses. These were different than the ones they were going to wear for the wedding. The men wore their tuxedos and I told them they needed to be careful since they had to use them again. Those suits were custom made. Since Nasir couldn't see me in my wedding dress, I wore a different one as well. Vera Wang made me this custom, white, lace gown and matching veil. It was beautiful, but the Ivory dress went better with the wedding decor. We took most of our pictures already.

Now it was time for just Nas and I to get a few at the top of the mountain. The group decided to stay down and wait for us. I begged Kiya to come with me, so I didn't have to be with him alone. Taking care of the kids was always my excuse back home, but this time it wasn't going to work. I don't know why I was so scared to ask him. If this was any other time, I would have called him as soon as I saw her, but something was different. I think because I was young and didn't have to be with him. I have ties to him but now we had a house, two kids, cars, and were a month away from getting married. Running was always my way to deal with things, but I was an adult with children; I couldn't do that anymore. I was afraid to ask him because I didn't want to hear that he fathered a child outside of our relationship. I would never be able to look at him again. Nasir would always leave out the same day and time but would never tell me where he was going. There was no way I could follow him when I had to drag a toddler and baby with me. Just getting them ready would take me over an hour. I had to be an adult and talk to him. My best friend was right.

"It's nice up here. Where did you even come up with this idea?" he asked me.

Looking out of the window, I could agree it was beautiful. We were higher than the mountains we skied on. The gang should have come up with us. If Cam and Callie were a little older, I would have loved to have them in some of the pictures with us. They were going to take some back home.

"Did you hear me?"

"My bad, I was thinking about something. Umm, I knew it wasn't going to snow back home, and I wanted snow in my wedding pictures since it's going to be on Christmas. I always wanted to come here, and this was the perfect opportunity," I replied.

"I think once Cam and Callie get older, we should come back every year around the holidays."

"Just us four?" I asked with a raised brow.

"Yea, who else would come? Our parents?"

"Maybe." I shrugged. "Let me ask you something."

"We are here. Watch your step when exiting," the ski lift announcer said.

Nasir helped me up and we stepped off. If I had heels on, I would be pissed because I would have fallen for sure. Since my feet were covered, I had on snow boots. We walked with the photographer for a few minutes until we stopped at the perfect spot to take pictures.

"What were you about to ask me?" Nasir questioned.

"We'll talk about it once we get back to the house. Let's get this over with because I have something planned back at the cabin," I changed the subject.

"Whatever."

While we were taking the last few pictures, it started to snow. These weren't little flakes either. I loved the snow.

"Can I get a few of you kissing in the snow?" Rayna, our photographer, asked.

Butterflies swarmed in my stomach. No matter what we went through, Nasir was the love of my life. Since the day I laid my eyes on him, I wanted to be with him. Shit changed when his mother moved in. I can admit most of my problems started when his she came. My frustration came from her talking to me like I was crazy and him not doing anything about it. And since he came back from Mexico, he's been a little distant. Something was on his mind, but he wouldn't tell me.

He held me by my waist and kissed me. We got a few shots like this before the snow became too much, and we decided to call it a wrap. I wasn't trying to be stranded on a mountain in the middle of a snowstorm. Grabbing my hand, we walked back to the lift and made small talk.

***

The lights danced around the small stage. I waited until the beat dropped before I started. The music played in the background.

"Christmas isn't for another month, but we are in the middle of a snowstorm, so I want to get everyone in the Christmas spirit. It's our first, annual, holiday karaoke night. So, I'm going to start it off singing one of my favorite holiday songs by my idol

Eartha Kitt," I said into the mic. "Santa baby just slip a sable under the tree for me. Been an awful good girl, Santa baby, so hurry down the chimney tonight."

I tried to do my best Eartha impression, making everyone laugh. It was funny, but I was in my zone. Christmas was my favorite time of the year. Especially singing along to my favorite songs. If I knew my friends would join, I would go around my neighborhood caroling the night before Christmas.

"Okay, it's my turn now," Kiya beamed.

She grabbed the mic from me, walked onto the stage and motioned for Crystal to join her. Kiya whispered something in her ear, and she grabbed another mic.

They sang TLC's "Sleigh Ride". Both of them did a dance which led me to believe this wasn't their first time reciting the song. We all stood up and cheered for them. I sang along because I knew every holiday song there was. When they were finished, Ava sang the infamous Mariah Carey song. Even the men sang along. This was a great idea to get everyone to do something together. The men liked to do their own thing or stayed in the game room playing Xbox or PlayStation.

"Let's go outside and have a snowball fight," Nasir suggested.

"I'm down," the men replied.

"We can do that, but if I tell y'all to stop then stop. Don't throw it in my face or head because it will be a problem," I told them.

After getting dressed in our warmest clothes, we went into the backyard. The snow was piling up, and I was excited. I hadn't played in the snow in over ten years. Winters weren't the same anymore. When I grew up, it snowed a lot every year, and we made snowmen and snow angels. The whole block used to have a huge snowball fight when school would get canceled.

"It's going to be girls against the guys," Kiya told them.

They agreed and both teams huddled up to talk about their game plan.

"We have an extra person on our team, so that gives us an advantage. The three of us can go against our men. Crystal, you lurk behind and hit them with a ball when they aren't paying attention," I lectured.

"Damn, bitch, it ain't that serious," Crystal replied.

"Yes, it is. They always win. It's our turn now," Ava said.

Crystal disappeared into the background, and we all went to find our spouses. Heem was distracted by something, and Kiya hit him in the back. Nasir was hiding behind trees, throwing snowballs. Each time I tried to catch up to him, I had to duck, so I wouldn't get hit.

"I'm going to get you," he said, coming from behind the tree.

I turned and ran, trying to dodge the balls coming my way. Running a little further than I meant to, I stopped in my tracks. There were a set of glowing eyes in the dark.

"Told you I was going to get you!" Nas yelled, out of breath.

"Stop. Look at that." I pointed.

When I said that, something with horns stepped out of the darkness. It was huge. Taller than Nas and I. I backed up into Nasir. He grabbed my arm and started running back towards the house.

"Slow down, I'm going to fall!" I shouted.

"Nahhh, fuck that. I'll stop when we get to the house. I don't need the rest of Santa's reindeer to pop up. Fuck this shit," he said, picking me up.

We yelled for the others to go into the house. Soon as we made it to the backyard, Nasir slipped on ice, and we both fell into a huge pile of snow. It couldn't stop laughing. I know we were going to be the topic of discussion for the rest of the night. Every time we all got together, they liked to bring up the time Nasir slipped when I was in labor.

"What the hell y'all running from?" Heem asked.

"It's some type of animal out there. It looked like a deer or something, but it was bigger than both of us," Nasir replied out of breath.

"Oh no. That's my cue to head inside," Crystal said.

"Yea, let's call it a night. Maybe we can all watch a movie or something," I told them.

***

Thanksgiving morning, I stood at the counter prepping the pies. They were going to be the last thing to go into the oven since they didn't take too long to cook. The men were watching the football game with the kids. Dinner was almost ready. We prepared the traditional Thanksgiving foods along with a few Jamaican foods. Ava made oxtails and curry chicken. My stomach was growling from smelling the delicious food. I couldn't wait to dig in.

"Jade, can you set up the table while I finish these yams?" Kiya asked me.

"Sure. Let me go grab the napkins from the pantry," I agreed.

After grabbing what I needed from the pantry, I noticed the napkins I wanted to use weren't in there. Then I remember Ava steamed them and left them in the laundry room. Placing the plates and forks down, I went to get the napkins. Before I could open the door, I heard Nasir in there whispering on the phone. Pressing my ear to the door to hear his conversation, I tried to listen for any clue of who he was talking to. He wrapped up his call, so I ran away from the door. I wondered who he was talking to in the laundry room. When we got back home, we needed to sit down and have a serious talk.

The kids sat at another table with their Nannies while the other adults talked amongst each other. I ate my food quietly. Looking around, I couldn't believe this was how my holidays were going. It seemed like yesterday I was in high school and spent the holidays with my own family. I wasn't in the best mood because all I could think about was Nasir and his secret conversations. What if he was calling to talk to his other son since we were out of town? This was the exact reason I should have listened to Kiya and been had this conversation over with. Here it was, Thanksgiving, and I was in a foul mood.

"Let's all go around the table and say what we are thankful for," Kiya announced.

One by one, everyone gave a heartfelt speech. I wasn't in the mood to contribute anything. I was pissed off and nothing was going to change that. The five glasses of wine didn't make it any better.

"I'm thankful for my beautiful fiancée and children," Nasir beamed.

I rolled my eyes and pushed my plate away. "How many children?" I asked, taking a sip of my wine.

"Jade, now is not the time," Kiya whispered.

I nodded my head because she was right. Now wasn't the time for me to be drunk and in my feelings.

Nasir looked at me with a raised brow before he continued. "I want to thank everyone for being a part of the wedding. From going on our trips to being up here in the cold. Thank you." He raised his glass.

"It's your turn, Jade," Ava said.

"No, she's fine," Kiya replied before I could say anything.

"Jade, let me talk to you in private," Nasir demanded.

I could tell he was upset by the expression on his face, but I didn't care. I wanted to sit here and finish the rest of my dinner, so I could take my tipsy ass to bed.

"I'm finishing my dinner before I go anywhere. Seems like you talk in private enough."

"What is that supposed to mean?" he asked me.

"Who were you talking to in the laundry room earlier?"

"We'll talk about it later. Hurry up and finish your food."

"Tell me now before you sneak away somewhere," I scoffed.

"The same shit can be said about you. You always say you're going to the gym, but I got a picture of you out with your ex sent to my phone, and I didn't say shit!" he shouted.

"My ex?" I was confused.

"Yes, your ex. The nigga who made a baby on you."

"Who, Donovan? I never went out with him!" I yelled.

"Then why are you in this picture smiling in his face?" He showed me the picture.

"Well, that is you, Jade. You have some explaining to do," Heem said.

"Mind your business!" Kiya snapped.

"Oh, so this is why you've been bugging every time I leave the house. Don't worry, I'm not a cheater like you," I chuckled.

"I haven't even looked at another woman since we've been back together. And even back then I never cheated on you, so I don't know why you continue to bring that shit up. We were not together when I was fucking with Mia, Ronnie, or Ashley, but you are a cheater though. You were fucking me while you were in a relationship with Daemon."

"Wow! You're going to bring a dead man into this?" I asked.

"What in the Tyler Perry's *Why Did I Get Married* is going on here?" Crystal asked, making me laugh.

It did remind me of that scene where everyone's secrets were exposed. But this was some real-life shit going on. Not a movie.

"You two need to go talk in private," Ava said to me.

"I just asked a simple question. Nasir, who were you talking to, and where do you sneak off to every Monday and Thursday?" I asked.

"Jad,e I promise you it's not what you think. I would never jeopardize what we have for anybody. Let's talk in private."

"Just tell me."

"Fuck it. I might as well tell everybody now. I have cancer."

Chapter Seven

Nasir

The look on Jade's face was something I couldn't describe. Her green eyes immediately filled with tears. I felt like shit keeping this from her, but I wanted to wait until I got some good news. I didn't want her to be stressed out before the wedding. It was a bad idea, but I thought I was doing the right thing at that time. This wasn't the way I wanted to let everybody know. Not like this. The look of pity on their faces was the exact reason I wanted to complete my treatment before letting them know.

"Okay, let's go talk in private," Jade said, standing up.

"Now you want to go after I've been telling you for that past few minutes."

She grabbed my hand, and we went into the room. I sat on the bed waiting for her to say something.

"Cancer. Nasir Miller? You are just now telling me you have fucking cancer. When did you find out?" she yelled.

"When I got back from Mexico."

"So, for a couple of months." She shook her head.

"Let me ask you something. Do you love me? Do you still

want to marry?" I asked her.

"Yes. Why would you ask me something like that?"

"Because you always think I'm cheating on you. I've been telling you that you mean the world to me, and I wouldn't mess that up for anyone. But you don't believe me. It's getting real tiring, Jade. If you always think I'm cheating, then maybe we shouldn't be getting married. We can still be together, but we should hold off on the wedding," I advised.

"A month away from the wedding and you want to call it off? If we don't get married next month then we are done for good."

"That's fine. You always have to be dramatic. All I said is we should wait. If you think I'm cheating on you, why would you even marry me? You want to get married because Kiya got married or because you love me?" I asked her.

"You are still that same asshole from back then," she replied and walked out.

***

It was the first of December, and I sat in my living room alone. When we got back, Jade took the kids and went to her parent's house. Shit was all fucked up. I should have never said what I said to Jade. Of course, I wanted to get married, but she had some issues she needed to work out. I loved Jade with every fiber of my being, but I didn't have time for her to accuse me of cheating every time I left the house. She was the one who got caught with her ex and still didn't explain why she was out with him. There was a knock on the door. I looked at my phone to see who was there. Kiya stood there waiting for me. I debated if I wanted to speak to her. I got up and went to open the door.

"Hey, Nasir," she smiled.

"What's good?" I replied.

I walked back to the living room and sat on the couch. She followed me, looking around the room.

"The wedding is in twenty-four days, Nasir. What the hell are you and Jade doing? Why is it so hard for you two to get it together?"

"I told her we needed to hold off on the wedding since she is always accusing me of cheating, and she was the one who told me we were done. Would you marry a man you accused of cheating on you? You know what, never mind. You and Heem went through the same shit," I chuckled.

"Real funny, Nas. But you two need to talk about it, so I can cancel everything and let people know the wedding is off."

"I know, but she won't talk to me. How is she doing? Did she ask about me?" I asked.

"Honestly, no. It's like nothing happened. Maybe she's putting on a front when I go see her. I'm going to talk to her tomorrow to see where her head is. But you were wrong for even suggesting calling the wedding off. You know how she is." Kiya sighed.

"It's always my fault, huh?" I smirked.

"Stop putting words in my mouth. You both are at fault all the time. Instead of talking to each other, y'all kept shit to yourselves. You think she was messing with her ex when that's far from the truth. Before we left for Bali, we went shopping and stopped for lunch. While I went to the bathroom, he stopped at the table and thanked her for not being a bitch and bad-mouthing him to his new girlfriend, which is her trainer Jill. Then he asked her something about proposing to his girl. That's why they were smiling in the picture. He and Jill are getting married in a few months thanks to Jade. Then Jade thought you had a baby with Dior. I need a damn break from y'all asses," she explained.

"A baby?" I choked.

"Yeah. We saw her that day at the mall and she had a little light skin baby who looked a little younger than Cam. I told her to talk to you when we first saw them. She overreacted a little but now that I think about it, I can't blame her. The little boy doesn't look shit like his mother and has the same complexion as you. Are you sure she wasn't pregnant?"

"Dior never told me about her being pregnant. If she was, don't you think she would have put me on child support? She was all about money and a baby would have been a great way to get it for the next eighteen years," I told her.

"True. But still, you two don't have the best history when it comes to you telling the truth about kids that may or may not belong to you. Go talk to her."

"I will after my surgery."

"When is it? Were you going to let Jade know?" she questioned.

"Why would I tell her? We aren't together anymore," I laughed.

"That shit is not funny. Text Heem, so he can go with you. I have to get out of here, but you need to talk to your fiancée and soon."

***

My mother has been calling my phone back-to-back but I didn't want to talk to her. A small part of this was her fault. I couldn't believe she had me thinking Jade was cheating on me. Communication played a huge part in why we weren't getting along. We needed to talk, but that was hard when she ignored my calls. If I wanted to see the kids, I had to go through her parents or Kiya. This wasn't how it was supposed to be. In a few more weeks, we were going to be husband and wife. Now, we were back at square one.

I laid in the bed scrolling through Dior's Facebook page. It's been on my mind ever since Kiya mentioned it. She looked good, but she still needed her ass beat for that shit she pulled with Jade. I stopped at a picture of her and the baby Kiya was talking about. It didn't look like me at all. The only similar thing was the skin, and that didn't mean shit. I got as far back as her baby shower. Some light-skinned dude was smiling in the pictures with her, so I assumed that was her baby father. I took a screenshot and sent it to Kiya to let her know I didn't have shit to do with her or her son.

It was a few days before my surgery and all I wanted to do was lay in bed and play my game all day and night. But that was going to have to wait until I finished my Christmas shopping. There were a few more items I needed to get for Jade. She wanted a new MacBook, phone, candles, and some other cosmetics. Jade already had more than enough shoes and clothes, so I didn't want to get her anymore. The kids had a bunch of toys and books. They were well taken care of and didn't need anything. The last stop of the day was to the Apple store. I looked around to see which one I could grab. They all looked the same to me, so I was a little confused.

"Do you need help finding anything?"

"Yes. I need the newest laptop that you have for my fiancée," I replied to the associate.

"That's going to be our 16-inch MacBook Pro. How much storage do you need?"

"Get me the one with the most and all of the accessories that goes with it," I told her.

Walking to the register, I waited while she got the laptop with the most storage and a mouse. It took a while, so I replied to a few texts. While I was waiting, I felt someone caress my arm. When I looked up, Dior was smiling on my face.

"Long time no see," she smirked.

"Not long enough," I said, wiping the smirk off of her face.

"Don't be like that, Nas. We used to get along well from what I can remember."

"That was before I found out you were a jealous, conniving bitch. You better be lucky Jade is not here because you would have gotten your ass beat."

"Where is your baby mother anyways?" She rolled her eyes.

"Home with our kids. We're getting married in a few weeks," I lied.

"I can't believe you strung me along while you were entertaining your ex."

"You can get the fuck out of my face with that bullshit right now. I don't give a fuck how you're feeling," I dismissed her.

This wasn't the time or place for her to be in her feelings. All I wanted to do was get these gifts and go home.

Chapter Eight

Kiya

Between Jade and her nonsense and me being sick, I was over it. I hope the new year starts off better than this. Since last night, I hadn't been feeling well. I was trying to lay off the meat so when I had a steak, it made me feel nauseous. Jade wanted to go last minute shopping and to pick up a gift she ordered for Nasir.

"Tell Jade she's going to have to go alone. You keep throwing up," Heem said, standing over me.

"No, I need to grab a few things too."

"The meat did this to you? It'll be funny if your ass is pregnant," he laughed, walking away,

Could I be pregnant? No way. The doctor said it would be difficult to do it alone. We stopped the treatment and talked about trying again in another year. I was still young and had enough time to stop for a while. Locking the door, I went into the cabinet and grabbed a pregnancy test. Pulling my pants down, I peed on the stick. I sat it on the counter and washed my hands. I waited and my stomach was in knots. Jade called me, and I told her I was on my way. Wrapping the test in tissue, I put it in my pocket and grabbed my coat and keys. I was too nervous to look at it.

We strolled through Greenwich looking for a jewelry store. Nasir wanted this watch and Jade had got it for him. She rambled about something, but I was thinking about the test in my purse. I don't know why I was so hesitant to look at it. Either I was pregnant, or I wasn't.

"Girl, are you listening to me?" Jade tapped my shoulder.

"Yes, Jade. Let's just get the watch and go home."

"No, you weren't. I said look at the store where we got our prom dresses. It was right before Nasir and Heem took us to the Bahamas for my birthday." She smiled, but it quickly disappeared.

"I remember," I smiled thinking about my husband. "What's wrong?"

"Nothing. The store is right here." She pointed at the sign.

Walking in, I noticed how upscale the place was. I wondered what kind of watch she was getting for him. He had a few Rolex watches, so I don't see why he needed a new one. Jade talked to the jeweler and I stood back looking at something that caught my eye. On an impulse, I ended up buying it. If I didn't need it, I would just sell it or give it away. Jade held up a small black bag and gave me a thumbs up. We walked back to the car and got in. Getting on the highway, I swerved in and out of traffic, trying to get home.

"Damn, don't kill me, I got kids to get home to."

"My bad," I said. "If Nas is your ex, why are you giving him a gift?"

"Because it's already paid for."

"Right," I smirked. "What did you get him?" I asked.

"One night we laid on the couch talking, and he mentioned

that he wanted two Patek watches. One with diamonds for when he wants to stunt on niggas and a regular one for when he's in a business meeting," she smiled.

"Why are y'all acting like this? The wedding is supposed to be in a few weeks. You need to take your ass home."

"I don't know. We were good one day then the next, we weren't. It's like we aren't meant to be together, but we're forcing it. This is the third time we tried this relationship thing, and it's not working. Maybe this is the end of us for good. I love him, but what if love isn't enough? I don't know, I'm over here rambling, not making any sense," she sighed.

"I talked to him, and he's missing you."

"Oh, so you fucking with the opps now?" she asked.

"Jade, please." I laughed. "You are being crazy. That's still my brother. We all have to get along, even if y'all not together."

"What was he talking about?"

"Just how he wants to talk to you, but you're not answering the phone." I rolled my eyes. "Stop ignoring him. I told him about everything, and he knows you weren't messing with Donovan, and that Dior's son is not his. It's that light-skinned dude P from the North son. Oh, and that he's having surgery tomorrow."

"Oh shit, I forgot he has the whole cancer thing going on. Damn, I'm really childish. I've been bothered by shit that isn't important when he's sick. Think it's about time for me to admit I am a bitch." She shook her head.

"I can't believe what I'm hearing right now," I teased.

"Shut up," she laughed.

We sat in silence for a few minutes, listening to music. I know she was beating herself up. Then I was carrying around pee on a damn stick because I'm scared to look at it for some reason. I think it was because I would be the only one who knew. Heem and I always looked at them together. We had each other to talk to it about. But this time, I would be all alone. It would be embarrassing to get my hopes up after I was the one to suggest we stop trying.

"I took a pregnancy test.," I blurted.

"When? What did it say?" Jade shouted.

"I don't know. I'm too scared to look at it. Heem doesn't know," I whispered.

"Where is it?" she asked.

"In my purse. Don't tell me what it says until I park the car."

She grabbed my purse and looked inside. Taking it out, she unwrapped it and turned her back against the window, so I couldn't try to look. I couldn't study her face because I had to focus on the road. Sneaking quick glances, I looked at her expression but couldn't make it out. Jade put her hand over her mouth and started to cry. Were they happy tears or tears of sadness? I looked for the next exit. I don't care if we were in Norwalk. I pulled into the Sono Collection parking lot and found the closest spot.

"What does it say?" I asked her.

She got out of the car and walked to the driver's side. My heart was beating rapidly, and I held my breath. Jade pulled me out and into a hug.

"We're having a baby!" she yelled.

I cried into her chest, "Let me see it," I said to her.

Looking at the test, there was the word *pregnant*. Just when I wanted to give up, God blessed me with another baby. I couldn't wait to tell Heem.

***

My doctor was able to squeeze me in the next morning. I prayed she was able to confirm I was indeed pregnant. I laid on the exam table flipping through a magazine.

"I thought you guys stopped trying?" the doctor asked.

"We did. I guess it happened the old-fashioned way." I shrugged.

"It's unusual for me to do an ultrasound so early in the pregnancy, but I want to see how far along you are since your periods are irregular."

I laid there looking at the screen, waiting for something to pop up. She moved it around a little more and a heartbeat was on the monitor. I smiled at the little fetus inside of me.

"From the looks of it, you're about eight weeks. Since it still is so early in the pregnancy, I want you to cut down your hours at the office and stay off of your feet. The heartbeat is nice and strong but keep your stress to a minimum. Continue to eat healthy, and I'm going to prescribe you some prenatal and iron pills. Come back in a month and after that, I want to see you every two-weeks."

I couldn't wait to tell Heem the good news, and I had the perfect way to announce it. We were late decorating, but I was super tired. He was in the shower while I got the baby dressed. Tonight, we were going to decorate our Christmas tree in matching pajamas. Once I was finished, I went downstairs to wait for him. I had a special ornament made and hid a small gift box in the box of ornaments.

"I'm staying in the house for the rest of the month. We'll order our groceries," Heem said, walking into the room.

"I already cut my hours at work. I'll be working twenty hours a week for a while. My notes can be done at home," I replied.

"Why? You just went back full-time," he said.

"With everything going on, I think it's best I spend more time at home. Plus, I have to go back to school if I ever want to be a dentist. You know I'm still a hygienist."

"Damn, you've been in school since we got together. You still not finished? Shit, at the rate you're going, Heemie's going to graduate before you," he laughed.

"No, he's not. I have two more years until I'm finished. Remember, I took time off to raise your big head baby."

"Ayyye, don't talk about my son's head like that. He got that shit from your big head father."

"Watch it," I laughed.

After we put the lights on the tree, it was time to put the ornaments on. I kept grabbing the regular ones, so Heem could hang the custom one. He kept missing it, and I didn't want to make it obvious.

"Who put this in here?" he held up the gift box.

"That's an early Christmas gift," I smiled.

"You are so extra. I didn't know we were exchanging gifts."

"We're not, but I wanted to get you something. Open it," I beamed.

I watched as his face looked over the diamond-encrusted pacifier pendant. When I saw it at the jewelry store with Jade, I knew it would make the perfect gift.

"Is this Heemie's gift or something?" he asked.

"No, Heem. It goes with this ornament." I showed him the one with my ultrasound picture on it.

He smiled and pulled me into a hug. "You're pregnant?"

"Yes, I confirmed it today. Last night when you said I could be pregnant, I took the test and had Jade look at it for me. I was too nervous and wanted to be sure before I told you. I'm eight weeks."

"I'm so happy. That's why you're cutting your hours back. Why don't you quit and go to school? You're not going to be able to do both. We have enough money. When you graduate, open your practice. You and Jade can go half."

"You make a good point. We could be the first black women to have our multi-doctor practice. If we hire other doctors, it can be a one-stop shop. I have to talk to her about it." I smiled.

This year started bad, but we were ending on a good note. Things were looking up for my little family. I prayed Jade's year was going to end the same way.

Chapter Nine

Jade

I sat in my closet trying to find something that fit me. Most of the clothes at my parent's house were small. I hadn't worn them in over five years. Instead of getting rid of this stuff like I told her to, my mother kept it all. Some of the items still had tags on them. Coming across a Pink sweatsuit and my UGGs, I put that on. It was the only loose-fitting clothing. Thinking about it, I was going to go through the stuff and keep certain things. Some of the clothes and shoes I had would be considered vintage when Callie got older. She would look cute in some of this stuff.

"When are you and your children going home?" my mother asked me.

"I am at home. You see I'm in my room," I replied.

"You moved out years ago. Your home is with Nasir. Cam has been crying to go home since you've been here. Jade, I love you and I don't mind y'all staying here, but you don't belong here sweetheart. You and Nasir built this amazing life, and you need to be enjoying it. With all this shit that is going on, I figured you would have learned life is too short to be acting like this. The wedding we all helped pay for is coming up, and you two aren't even living in the same house."

"But-" I interrupted her.

"But nothing!" she scolded. "You are too fucking grown to be still throwing these temper tantrums like a damn child. I blame your father for that shit. I let you do what you want because at the end of the day you're a grown woman, but I'm not about to let you ruin your life. Especially since you have my grandchildren to think about. When you come back, I will have all of your stuff packed and ready."

"Wow! I can't believe you're kicking me out. I'm going to tell my daddy," I pouted.

"Who do you think sent me up here? We both agree you need to go home and work things out with the father of your children. We love you, but it's time to be an adult," she said before leaving out.

Everybody was getting on my damn nerves. Kiya washed her hands of me and now my parents were doing the same thing. I knew they all were right; I was being a brat. When I didn't get my way, I wasn't trying to hear shit. Nasir told me he had cancer, and I ignored him and ran away like always. Every night before bed, I prayed he was okay. So many times, I wrote a text but erased it. That was my foolish pride. After wiping away the few tears that managed to escape, I turned the car off and walked into the hospital. According to the front desk, he was already out of surgery. They had a cancelation, and he came in earlier. I was kind of sad because I wanted to be here before they started. Walking to the elevator, I pressed the button. Someone was waving for me to hold it, but I continuously pressed the close button. With Ms. Rona going on, I wasn't taking any chances with this shit. Before this shit started, I hated to be in a tight space with strangers. I stopped at the nurse's station, and they told me to go to the room.

When I walked in, he was sleeping. Walking over to him, I leaned over and hugged him. I started to cry because I felt so guilty. Anything could have happened to him, and I was too busy being a bitch.

"What are you doing? I'm trying to sleep." He pushed me off of him.

"I'm sorry for not being here. I wanted to be here before the surgery, but they changed the time. Why didn't you tell me?" I asked him.

"We're not together anymore, I don't have to tell you anything." He shrugged.

"Who said we weren't together? I wanted to give you your space since you called off the wedding. My stuff is back home," I lied.

"Jade, when we were in Aspen, you told me that if we didn't get married, we were done. I swear your ass is bugged out."

"I don't recall that, but I guess I said it since that's what you remember."

"It's the truth."

"Okay, whatever." I rolled my eyes "I understand if you don't want to marry me, and I am okay with that. I'll just be your girlfriend and baby mother for the rest of my life."

"Don't start, Jade. I just got out of surgery, and I need to rest," he said to me.

"Go to sleep then." I rolled my eyes.

"Why are you like this?" he asked me.

"Listen here. I've had enough of you, my parents, and Kiya coming for me. I'm here trying to mend our relationship or whatever this is. Take your ass to sleep. You wanted to rest so go ahead. I'll be here when you wake up," I told him.

He closed his eyes, and I left the room to go find his doctor.

I needed to know what went on with his surgery. Walking over to the nurse's station, I called for someone to help me.

"What can I help you with?" the pretty nurse said.

"I would like to talk to my husband's doctor." I smiled.

"Which patient is he?"

"Nasir Miller."

"He's married? I didn't see a ring on his finger," she said louder than she should have.

"Look, can you tell the doctor that his wife is here, and I'll be in his room waiting to talk to him?" I snapped.

When I walked back into the room, he hurried up and closed his eyes. I wanted to go over there and yank his ass out of the bed, but I wanted to be on my best behavior since everybody had a problem with the way I behaved. I let him slide for now. Ten minutes later, a handsome older guy walked in.

"It's nice to finally meet you, Mrs. Miller." He extended his hand.

"It's Ms. Chen. I wish I could say the same. Nasir told me he had cancer on Thanksgiving." I cut my eyes to him still pretending to be asleep.

"I told him he needed to tell his family, but he was too stubborn. I am here to answer any questions."

I listened as the doctor explained to me that he found cancer early and was able to treat it with chemotherapy. The surgery was to see if there was any cancer left or if it spread. They didn't see anything which meant he was going to be okay.

"Even though Mr. Miller is in the clear, we still want him to come in for routine blood work every six months just to make sure it's gone for good," the doctor continued.

"Wow! Thank you. Can I have your business card?" I asked him.

Nasir was able to keep his diagnosis from everybody, but I was going to make sure that wasn't going to happen again. I needed to be added as a medical contact person so I could call his doctor and get information. This whole situation was stressful. From the unnecessary bickering to him keeping something like this from me, it was exhausting.

"Here you go. I'll be in contact soon to set up the first appointment." He handed me his card.

Sitting down, I pulled out my iPad and went to my Kindle app. This was considered my quiet time, and I wanted to catch up on some reading. Nasir was sleeping, and I was halfway through my book when the door opened. When I looked up, my eyes landed on Miranda. I was going to keep my mouth shut because this was her son. As long as she didn't say shit to me, I was fine. Ignoring her, I focused my attention back on my book.

"Can you give me private time with my son? I'm sure you have somewhere to be," she said to me.

"He is sleeping. What can you possibly need privacy for? I'm reading my book, so you can say what you want," I said to her.

"I don't even know why you're here. It's not like he's going to marry you. At this point, you're just his baby mother, and I'm the one who gave birth to him," she smirked.

I know it gave her satisfaction to say that shit, and she was right, so I wasn't going to reply to that. There was plenty of things I needed to do and beating the shit out of Nasir's mother wasn't on my to-do list. Instead of me going back and forth with her, I was going to go home to avoid me getting arrested. Grabbing my bag, I got up so I could get my kids and go home.

"That's what I thought," she said.

I was doing so good until she said that. Counting to five, I tried to calm down to avoid doing something I was going to regret.

"Listen here, bitch, I let a lot of your slick comments slide, but you got me fucked up today. Even though we're not getting married, I'm still the main bitch in his life. If it wasn't for me, your ass wouldn't even be around. He hated you, but I told him that no matter what you did, you were still his mother. A bad mother, but still his mother. You spent his childhood chasing dick and not taking care of him. Keep up that nasty ass attitude and you won't be around my kids. I don't give a fuck what your son says. My children will not be around someone who constantly disrespects me, family or not. So, I suggest you tread lightly before you are paying your own bills. I may not be his wife, but I do control the money. And if you got something else to say, let's go outside so we can handle that!" I shouted, poking her in her forehead.

"I can't wait to tell my son how you behaved."

"Girl, what the fuck is he supposed to do? Just watch your mouth or next time I'm going to pop you in it," I told her before walking away.

**

My mom wasn't playing. When I got to the house, all of the kids' stuff was ready by the door. She was right though. At home with Nasir is where I belonged. He had a small incision so he was coming home tomorrow, and the room could be used for someone who needed it. The kids were sleeping, so I took this as a chance to start wrapping the gifts. They were stored in a room so the kids wouldn't see them. We were going to leave homemade cookies out for Santa and when the kids went to sleep, we were going to place all of the gifts under the tree. It made it seem more real.

When I was growing up, my parents placed all of the gifts under the tree throughout the month. My uncle kind of ruined Santa for me. When we were at my grandmother's house in the hood, spending Christmas with her, he told me Santa got shot off the roof with an AK-47 and that's why they put the gifts out early. I don't know why I believed his drunk ass. That story didn't even make sense. I missed his drunk ass. He passed away a few years back. I stayed up for a few more hours before I called it a night. My back was killing me from leaning over.

The sun shined through the window and the brightness woke me up. I forgot to close the curtains last night. Looking at my phone, I noticed it was a little later than I usually got up. Looking at the baby monitors, both of the kids were still sleeping. Dragging myself out of the bed, I went to the bathroom to take a quick shower. For some reason, I was tired as hell. Hopefully, this shower woke me up. After my shower, I put on a red Fenty lounge set. I checked on Callie and Cam before I went to start breakfast. Nasir was coming home, and I wanted him to have something to eat when he walked through the door.

"Somebody slept late." Nasir smiled at me.

"What are you doing here so early?" I asked.

"I had them discharge me earlier. They gave me pain meds, so I'm doing okay. Breakfast is already finished. When they get up, I'll feed Cam, so you can get Callie ready."

"You had surgery, let me handle the kids. We can all sit in the living room and watch movies together."

"Sounds like a plan. I'm going to take a shower and put on something comfortable."

The Grinch played on the TV. Cam sat on the floor staring at it. He only liked to watch his favorite cartoons, but this movie kept his interest. Callie was snuggled in her father's arms, playing with his beard. I was trying to write the perfect email to some of the wedding vendors. It was embarrassing as hell to cancel so close to the date. I should have let Kiya do this when she asked me.

"What are you over there doing on your phone?" he asked me.

"Emailing the people to let them know the wedding is canceled." I shrugged.

"We need to talk about that. If you want to, we can still get married."

"You don't have to marry me because you feel sorry for me. Honestly, I don't even care at this point. You were right, we shouldn't get married."

"So, now you don't want to marry me?" he questioned.

"Nope. I'm good, love," I chuckled. "You already told me you didn't want to get married, and I understand that, babe. Deep down inside, I knew you weren't ready to get married. I'm surprised you even wanted more kids."

"So, what are you trying to say?"

"You have commitment issues. It's been this way since we met. I'm used to it, but we can try again in another eight years."

"Look, I love you, Jade, but you always assume I'm doing something that I'm not. That's why I suggested we hold off on the wedding. For you. I still want to marry you, and I always have. You mean the world to me. I just need you to trust me. Why would you want to marry someone you don't trust?"

"I get what you're saying, and I can understand why you said what you said. You don't have the best track record with other women, and that's why I said you're right. We don't need to get married right now. Maybe we can go to counseling or something," I suggested.

"Everything is paid for and all of our family is going to be here. I don't care what you say, we're getting married this Christmas. I should have never said we shouldn't get married. Plus, I need my wife to be someone who stands up for herself. I heard what you said to my mother. I promise you don't have to deal with her again."

"She was lucky I had to pick the kids up. I was going to wait for her outside and beat her ass. I tried to get along with her, but that's never going to happen," I told him.

"That's fine with me. You were the one who wanted me to talk to her so bad. Now you see why I loved her miserable ass from a distance," he laughed.

"I get in now."

"So, are we still getting married?" he asked.

"I don't know."

Chapter Ten

Nasir

"If I was Jade, I wouldn't be so quick to marry your ass either. You had no business telling that girl that. Now, you don't want to go see a therapist with her," my grandmother fussed.

"All I'm saying is why do we need to go see a marriage counselor if we're getting married in a couple of weeks?"

"Y'all need to go see one because your relationship is rocky. It started because of your evil ass mama. Jade tells me everything. It took you long enough to put her in her place. How is she going to try to come around after all of these years and tell you how to run your life? If it was up to me, her ass wouldn't be allowed at the wedding. Talking to someone is the right thing to do, even after you get married. These problems aren't going to go away after you say I do."

"I hear you. I'll go," I sighed.

"You didn't have a choice in the matter. Go home and spend time with your family."

"Okay. Are you still staying the night on Christmas eve?" I asked her.

"No. I told you my friend is coming over here, and we are

going to open our gifts together."

"What friend? And I don't recall you telling me that. Is he more important than your family?"

"Nasir, don't do that when I'm grown. You and Heem both have your family, and I'm over here lonely. I need to have someone too."

"You can live with me. We live in that big ass house, and the kids would love to see you every day," I told her.

"I will keep that in mind when I get a little older, but Grandma needs her space and privacy right now."

"I understand, but I'm going to get out of here. I love you."

***

It was two days before Christmas, and we sat at a table in a hall. My friend Amir and his baby mother Aaliyah were throwing a small holiday party for the kids. I met him a few years ago and it turned out that Jade and Kiya knew his baby mother and her friends. When you walked in there was a balloon garland with candy canes and shiny red balloons. The tables had red, white, and green tablecloths and chair covers. The centerpieces were mini-Christmas trees with ornaments and the guests' names on them. There were life-size gingerbread house cutouts that had activities for the kids inside. Santa's chair was located near the treat tables. It was nice as hell, and Cam was already running around.

"Wow! Aaliyah, this place looks beautiful," Jade smiled at her.

"Thank you. It took forever to set all this shit up. I can't wait till the holidays are over because I'm exhausted."

The men were by the makeshift bar, and I made my way over to them. I didn't want to get caught up in their conversation about decorations.

"What's good, Amir?"

"Nothing much. Getting ready for Christmas, and your wedding. It would be you to have a wedding on a major holiday. Shit, I'm already going to be tired from this big dinner Aaliyah is having tomorrow," he sighed.

"Jade just wants us to spend the night with the kids watching Christmas movies and bake cookies," I replied.

"Lucky you. She's in the Christmas spirit this year, and she is trying to outdo one of her old friends. They're both having parties tonight." He shook his head.

"I know how that goes," I laughed.

Smiling, I looked around at everybody having a good time. Christmas music played and the kids were feeding reindeer carrots. This is what we all needed. A fun night with no worrying or arguments. 2020 has been a hectic year from Covid-19 to the drama between Jade and I. Going into the New Year, I wanted it to be drama-free. I tried to make it work with my mother, but I wasn't going to allow her around if she didn't respect Jade. Hearing my grandmother co-sign on my feelings let me know I was making the right choice. Jade came first. Even though my mother was related to me by blood, it didn't mean anything. Jade came into my life and turned it around. If it hadn't been for her, I would have still been in the streets, sleeping with multiple women. Now, I had a woman who meant the world to me, and two happy, healthy children.

"Two more days and you'll be a married man. Are you ready?" Heem asked me.

"I been ready."

"Y'all just got back together for the fifth or sixth time," he laughed.

"I know you're not laughing because there was a time when Kiya almost canceled y'all second wedding. And she kicked you out of the house."

"Damn, calm down. I thought we were the only group of friends that had a bunch of shit going on," Monte joked.

"I could write a fucking book on the shit we been through." I shook my head.

"They have a pool table in the back. Let's grab some beer and play a few games before the women come looking for us," Amir said.

We played a few games of pool before we went to join our families. It was time for Santa to take pictures with all of the kids. Callie looked at him and screamed. I grabbed her and sat back at our table. Jade took a picture with Cam and Santa. Taking out my phone, snapped a few of my own. Jade was going to want to post them later. We ate dinner and played a few games before both Cam and Callie started to get tired.

***

This was the first Christmas in a while where I was truly happy. I was excited to see the faces of my family. We were extremely blessed but were appreciative when we got gifts. It was the night before Christmas, and we sat around the table decorating cookies while Christmas music played in the background. Jade was an amazing baker. She made two dozen sugar cooks and homemade icing.

"You have to do it like this, Cam." Jade guided his small hand.

"He's making a mess," I laughed.

"I'm going to have to change his pajamas. I should have waited to give him a bath," she said, kissing his cheek.

"My cookies look way better than yours," I teased.

"Please, Nasir. Your snowman cookie looks like the sun came out and melted his ass. And is that a carrot nose or a bell pepper?" she laughed.

"You got jokes, huh?" I chuckled.

"You're the one lying about your cookies. I think this is enough cookies. I'm going to wipe him off, and we can watch movies in the living room."

Jade got up and I went into the living room to turn on that new Christmas movie with a black cast. It was called *Jingle Jangle*. I think this was going to be our tradition from now on. I couldn't wait until the kids got older and were able to enjoy this.

"This little boy is something else. Cam, go sit with your father."

"Come here, Lil man." I held out my arms.

We snuggled on the couch and watched the first 40-minutes of the movie before the kids went to sleep. I grabbed them and went to tuck them into their beds. Jade was still into the movie, and I laid my head on her lap. She played with my beard while keeping her eyes on the TV.

"I want you to open up one of your gifts," she said and handed me a box.

Tearing the wrapping paper off, I smiled at the box. I knew what was inside. When I opened the box, I was surprised. There were two Patek watches. One with diamonds and one without. A few months ago, we were laid on the couch how we were now, and I told her I wanted two of them. This was why I loved her. When I thought she wasn't paying attention, she remembered what I wanted. Yeah, I had enough money to buy them myself, but I didn't think it was that important and was going to wait.

"Thank you. I can't believe you remembered what I said all of those months ago." I got up and kissed her. "I got you something too."

She grabbed the small square box and opened it. Her eyes widened as she looked at the new engagement ring I got for her. The old one was nice, but there was too much bad energy connected to it. This one was bigger and cost more. She deserved it.

"A new ring already? We didn't even get married yet."

"I figured I'll get you a new ring."

"You didn't have to, but I appreciate it. I'll save this one for Callie," she said, taking off the old ring.

We watched the movie until Jade went to sleep. I carried her to the room and covered her up. While everyone was sleeping, I placed all of the gifts under the tree and went to cuddle with Jade.

***

We sat around the table with a cup of whiskey. This was the day everybody was waiting for. Me and Jade were finally getting married. We've been meeting with a therapist twice a week to make sure we were on the same page. I was happy that today was the day I would marry the girl of my dreams. We've been through a lot over the years, and I was happy we were making it official.

"We have a few more minutes until it's time for him to head to the altar. Hopefully, Jade will make it," Heem laughed.

"Shut the fuck up!" I snapped.

"You better watch what you say. The preacher somewhere around here," Zeek said.

"I don't give a fuck. If his ass wants to get paid, he better keep his mouth shut until it's time for the ceremony."

"I know I didn't just hear that," my grandmother said.

"I'm sorry, but these two in here getting on my nerves," I laughed.

"It's time, baby. Jade is almost ready."

This was it. I was almost a married man. We all stood and headed to where the ceremony was taking place. It was my first time seeing the decorations, and I was impressed. Jade told me how she wanted it, but I never paid attention. The guest smiled at me, and I nodded my head at a few of them. One by one, the girls walked out to a song by Aaliyah. Next up was Cam who was the ring bearer, then two flower girls came out dropping red rose petals. We both wanted Callie to be included in the wedding, so Zeek's son pulled her in a wagon that was turned into a sled. Everyone cooed as they saw her. Callie clapped her hands together and laughed. The doors opened again. Jade and her father stepped onto the white and gold runner. Tears welled up, and I wanted to cry. Although I couldn't see her face, I knew she looked beautiful. I smiled and waited for her to reach me.

Chapter Eleven

Jade

I didn't mean to fall asleep on Nasir last night, but I was so comfortable and at peace for the first time in months. Looking over, Nasir was still sleeping, so I got up and went to get breakfast started. It was 8:00 a.m. and the kids were going to be up in the next hour or so. I prepared Christmas themed pancakes, sausage, eggs, and grits. Nasir didn't care for pancakes, so I made him steak and home fries. Looking down at my new ring, I smiled. God blessed me with a wonderful man. Sometimes I questioned if we were meant to be together because of our fights, but when I looked at all the good things, they outweighed the bad. Nasir was the man for me. My phone started to ring, and I went to find it. Kiya was calling me.

"Hello," I answered.

"Good morning, and Merry Christmas bride-to-be."

"Morning, Babe," I smiled.

"Did you guys open your gifts yet?" she asked.

"They are still sleeping. I'm cooking breakfast before they get up. I rather let them sleep a little later, so they can wake up to food. We have to leave here in about two hours to head to the venue," I told her.

"I know. We opened our gifts. I was talking to the venue and making sure all of the vendors are setting up. Most of the decorations are up and it looks breathtaking, Jade. I thought you were bugging with this whole Christmas theme, but I will remember this for years to come."

"Thank you. I had to be different, but I'll call you in about an hour. I think Cam is up."

When I hung up, Nasir was coming down the stairs with both kids. I smiled and Cam ran into my arms.

"Merry Christmas, my love." I kissed his cheek.

"It smells good down here. I'm starving," Nasir said, rubbing his stomach.

"The food is finished. We can eat first."

Once we finished eating, we went into the living room. Cam went crazy looking at all the presents piled high. I sat on the floor holding Callie why Nasir handed Cam his gifts and helped him open them. I opened Callie's gifts for her. She was still young, so she wasn't as excited. Nasir opened the other gifts I got him and thanked me.

"Let me get Callie while you open yours."

All of my gifts were put to the side, and I started opening them. He got me a new phone, Macbook, iPad Pro, bags, shoes, and the last gift was in an envelope.

"What's this?" I asked, looking at the papers.

"Me and Heem went half and purchased you and Kiya a building. When y'all finally finish school, we want y'all to open your own practice. Why work for someone when you and your best friend can build something?"

Out of all of my gifts, I think this was my favorite. I loved getting material things, but this was something that was the start of me having my medical practice. People worked for years to be able to do that. I wasn't finished with my degree just yet, but my man got me a building. After the wedding, I was going to talk to Kiya about having other doctors work for us, so we didn't have the building sitting there collecting dust.

"I don't know what to say," I cried.

He pulled me into a hug and kissed me on the forehead. "You don't have to say anything. I love you, Jade."

We spent the next hour cleaning up so we could give the kids their baths and head to the venue. We were getting married at the Aria in Prospect, CT. It was kind of far, but everyone was able to get there in the shuttles we rented. Most of our family from out of town stayed in hotels closer to the venue. The first thing I went to do when I got to the venue was to make sure everything was how I wanted it. Where the ceremony was taking place was very minimal since we weren't going to spend a lot of time there. The room was dimly lit and candles lined the aisle along with tall white trees with crystals hanging from them. Clear Chiavari was 6-ft apart to give the guests enough space. We were saying our vows under a flower canopy.

"I think I want a natural glam," I told the makeup artist.

"What about a gold and brown smokey eye with a burgundy lip since it's a Christmas theme. It would go great with the ivory dress as well," she replied.

"Sounds good."

The girls' makeup and hair were finished. The ceremony was in less than an hour and the only thing I had to do was finish getting my makeup applied and put on my dress.

"I can't believe we made it here. Jade and Nasir are finally getting married." Crystal held up her glass.

"I know your ass ain't tipsy already." I laughed.

"No, I'm not, but I can't wait to down some Patron. We're going to party like it's 1999," she chuckled.

"Yup, this bitch feeling nice. Girl, give me this glass." Kiya snatched the champagne.

"What? It's never too early to celebrate," Ava laughed.

"Yes, the hell it is. We have about an hour and a half to get through," I told them.

"You never told me if you two were writing your vows," Kiya said.

"No. We both wanted to go the traditional route and you know Nasir wasn't going to speak from the heart in front of all of those people."

"That's what me and Zeek did. I didn't want to have to do those speeches in front of everybody. Too much," Ave said.

"I'll probably get hitched like Kiya. I don't think I want a big wedding. It's not enough people to even come if I get married." Crystal shook her head.

"You are right about that. The family can't stand your ass," Kiya joked.

"Hush," I told them.

Half an hour later, I was stepping into my dress. The satin ivory gown fit my body like a glove at the top. I wanted a ball gown instead of the usual mermaid gown.

"Can someone get my shoes?" I asked.

"I'll get them," Kiya said. "Oh my God, Jade, you have the

Manolo Blahnik shoes Carrie Bradshaw married Mr. Big in."

"I knew you would get the relation. This is why I got the satin dress in the same color as her original dress but in a different style."

"That's right. How iconic." She smiled.

"You know how I do." I winked at her.

I looked in the mirror and couldn't believe I was finally about to get married. Eight years of murder, lies, cheating, and drama, I was finally getting my happily ever after with the man of my dreams.

"Look at my baby. You look absolutely beautiful." My mother hugged me.

"Wow! Let me get a picture," Crystal said, taking out her phone.

The girls left the suite. It was just me and Kiya sitting around, waiting for our turn to go out.

"Are you nervous?" she asked me.

"A little. And I don't know why when we live together and have a family already," I sighed.

"You're waiting on the other shoe to drop. When things are going great, you like to think of all the things that can mess that up. You deserve to be happy, so be happy. Don't think about something bad happening. And if it does, you work that shit out. Marriage is not easy; you have to work at it every single day," she lectured.

"I understand, but you never had the problems we did. Since I met him, we've been through nothing but bullshit with a few females."

CHRISTMAS WITH THE MILLERS

"Then don't marry him if you're always going to bring that up. He was right when he told you to wait to get married. Whatever happened in the past needs to stay there. When you two are having problems, you can't always bring that shit up."

"I know. That's my only problem. He's a great boyfriend and father."

"And he was right. He never cheated on you."

"Kiya, it's your turn," my father said to her.

She kissed my cheek and left out. I sat on the chair trying to calm my nerves. This was what I wanted but marriage was a huge step. Even when I moved away and tried to forget about Nasir, he was all that I thought about. The distance didn't make me miss him any less. Daemon was a placeholder for the man I wanted to be with. If I would have never tried to play it off, I would have never put my life in danger.

This was it. I was going to be Mrs. Nasir Miller in less than twenty minutes. My father walked back in and held his hand out for mine. We walked to the entrance to the hall, and I linked my arms in his.

"I don't always get into your business because you're an adult, but Nasir is the man for you. He reminds me a lot of myself when I was younger. I know you two haven't had the best record, but people make mistakes. Me and your mother had our fair share of problems, but we worked hard for our relationship," my father said.

"What problems have you two had?" I asked.

I could never recall my parents having any problems. Growing up, I had the best childhood with both of my parents in the house. We didn't always live in a big house but that didn't matter because I had my parents.

"When you were around three or four, your mother took you and went to stay with your grandmother for two months. I had to jump through hoops just to get her to talk to me."

"Well, what did you do?" I asked.

"Some things are better left unsaid, but we were able to work on it, and we've been fine ever since. And your mother doesn't bring it up like you do to him."

"How do you know what I do to him?" I questioned.

"He tells me at our weekly golf game."

"I didn't know you two hung out."

"When you moved away, we started to hang out, but then he moved away. I like him, Jade. He's a great guy, and he'll make a wonderful husband. I always prayed you would marry a guy that was able to take care of you the way I do. Nasir does that and more."

I smiled and replayed our conversation. Never did it think my parents had any relationship trouble, but I was wrong, and it made me more confident. I was going to ask my mother all about it. Her ass wouldn't hesitate to tell me what happened. Pulling my veil over my face, I held the bouquet tightly. Aaliyah's song "Turn the Page" played, and we stepped foot onto the carpet. Everyone stood up and looked my way. My eyes were on Nasir the whole way. I could tell he wanted to cry but was trying to keep the tears at bay.

"Who gives this woman to be married to this man?" the officiant said.

"I do." My father smiled, he kissed me on the cheek.

"You look beautiful." Nasir mouthed.

"Thank you," I replied.

On December 25th, 2020, Nasir and I officially became husband and wife. I took a few pictures with my guests in my wedding dress before I changed into something more comfortable. I wanted to match the decorations of the reception. Kiya picked out a Valentino floral lace gown with a tulle overlay. It was a little pricey, but she gave it to me as a wedding gift. The guests were being seated so me and Nasir could walk in as husband and wife.

"There is no turning back now. You really married my ass," Nasir joked.

"You're not that bad." I winked.

"Everybody, welcome Mr. and Mrs. Nasir Miller," Heem announced.

Jagged Edge's "Let's Get Married" played, and we walked in holding hands. Everyone clapped as we made our way to the middle of the floor. The wedding party was dancing, and we joined them. Even the guests joined in. This was why I didn't want a slow song playing. I wanted this to be a celebration from the very beginning. Once the song went off, we sat at our table so we could get a few pictures.

Our table was surrounded by the wedding party. Candles with red roses decorated the table. I wanted it to be simple since there was a huge wall made of fresh roses and greenery behind us. The tables the guests sat at were covered in ivory tablecloths. For the centerpieces, I wanted small, fresh Christmas trees with red and white roses in them. Small, gold ornaments with our name and date were written in Swarovski crystals for the guests to take home as favors. Around the room, there were strategically placed Christmas trees with the same roses at the centerpieces. Off to the side of our table was the cake. The ten-tier cake sat on a gold chandelier that hung from the ceiling. The gift table was filled to the top. I was happy our family and friends weren't the type to show up empty-handed. Most people showed up empty-handed and to be nosey or judge the event. My mother joked and said she was going to be at the door to make sure everybody came with something. Most of the stuff that was on the registry was for the house that I didn't buy. And someone at the venue suggested that we put our honeymoon on there to get people to pay for it. I shrugged it off, but I was happy I did because a few days after I sent everyone the link, I got a notification that our trip was paid for. I think Kiya and Heem paid for it.

"This came out nice. How much did all of this cost?" Nasir asked me.

"The price of a 2020 G-Wagon."

"I figured it was around that much. It was worth it though."

"I know. I'm happy we did it on Christmas," I told him.

"Me too. It's different."

"Dance With My Father" by Luther Vandross came on, and that was my cue to grab my father's hand. We danced around and everyone recorded and took pictures. I closed my eyes and put my head on his chest. When I was younger, we used to always listen to this song and my father told me he wanted to dance at my wedding to it. I wouldn't have any other song playing at this very moment. Before Nasir, my dad was the number one man in my life. Opening my eyes, my mother stood to the side crying. I motioned for her to join us. At this moment, I wanted to cry. It was like something you saw in a romance movie. The song went off and Nasir grabbed my hand, pulling me close to him by my waist.

"You know I love you, right?" he asked me.

"I know and I love you more. Always did and always will."

"Well, it's been five years, can't hold back my tears 'cause I'm just so happy I'm marrying an angel today. Oooo…"

When I turned around and saw Jamie Foxx singing, I almost passed out. I always said I wanted him to sing this song at my wedding when I was younger. Kiya and I loved *The Jamie Foxx* show when we were kids. I always said I wanted him to sing the song he sang to Fancy on their wedding day.

"Surprise," Kiya whispered to me.

"Nasir, I can't believe you did this," I cried.

"Anything to make you happy, my love."

Once Jamie was finished, we took pictures with him before he had to leave. We danced and drank all night long. It was almost the end, and I wanted to throw the bouquet so we could leave for our honeymoon. I walked to the top of the stairs.

"I need all of the single ladies to head to the middle," I announced.

About thirty women got up, and I was shocked at how many unmarried females were in my family. Crystal was front and center. I knew she was going to show out. After the count of three, I threw it, and Crystal jumped in the air to catch it before it even hit the ground.

"Rashad, we next baby." She pointed at him, making everybody laugh.

Nasir and I made our rounds to say goodbye to everyone before we left out. The kids were staying with my parents until we got back. Kiya agreed to help them out if they needed it.

"I'm so happy for you, best friend. Make sure to call me and tell me about everything." Kiya hugged me.

"Thank you. I'll call you soon as the flight lands to let you know we made it. Remember, you need to rest," I scolded her.

Nasir grabbed my hand and led me to the limo. We were taking a private jet to St. Lucia where we were staying for a week. I would have loved to stay longer but being away from my babies longer than a week wasn't happening.

***

We sat on the beach looking at the crystal-clear water, holding hands. I was in heaven. We finally got married after eight years. This is where I was destined to be.

"I love you, Nasir," I said to him.

"I love you more." he kissed me.

The End

To submit a manuscript to be considered, email us at submissions@majorkeypublishing.com

Major Key Publishing is accepting submissions from experienced & aspiring authors in the areas of Contemporary Romance, Urban Fiction, Paranormal, Mystery & Suspense & New Adult Romance!

If interested in joining a successful, independent publishing company, send the first 3-5 chapters of your completed manuscript to submissions@majorkeypublishing.com

Submissions should be sent as a Microsoft Word document, along with your synopsis and contact information.

WWW.MAJORKEYPUBLISHING.COM

Be sure to LIKE our Major Key Publishing page on Facebook!

Made in the USA
Coppell, TX
25 October 2023